CAPTIVITY

To escape being married off to a rich man—any rich man!—by her snobbish and ambitious mother, Alex fled to Melbourne, only to meet someone who was just as determined as her mother had been. Chase Marshall offered her marriage as well—but Alex was under no illusions as to why: he simply thought she would be suitable. Well, he could keep his offer of marriage!

CAPTIVITY

BY

MARGARET PARGETER

MILLS & BOON LIMITED
15–16 BROOK'S MEWS
LONDON W1A 1DR

First published 1981
Australian copyright 1981
Philippine copyright 1981
This edition 1981

© Margaret Pargeter 1981

ISBN 0 263 73473 0

Set in Monophoto Times 10 on 11 pt

Made and printed in Great Britain by
Richard Clay (The Chaucer Press), Ltd.,
Bungay, Suffolk

CHAPTER ONE

THE flat in the Fitzroy district of Melbourne was, to Alex Latham, the last word in luxury. True, it wasn't very large, but for the two girls who shared it, it was more than adequate. Alex didn't know how Ruby Marshall, the other girl, could complain as she was doing now, with such an air of martyrdom, that there was barely room to swing a cat.

'I'm going mad!' Ruby exclaimed, flinging up her dark head dramatically. 'Everything gets lost!'

Obligingly Alex dived under Ruby's bed, extracting her missing evening slipper. 'If you'd only learn to be a bit tidier, Ruby, you wouldn't think you were going mad at all.'

Ruby moaned, quite seriously, 'How can I be expected to learn new habits at my age?' Accepting her shoes without a word of thanks, she sat down to put them on. The buckle caught on her fine silk stockings and she cast Alex another dour glance.

Alex returned the look wryly. The only time Ruby ever referred to her age was when she wished to avoid doing something. 'I thought you came to Melbourne to learn to stand on your own two feet?'

'So what?' snapped Ruby. 'Surely that has nothing to do with being tidy?'

Ruby could be sharp when she liked. Alex thought she could have made a list of things that might have improved Ruby's personality—such as learning to be more agreeable to those less favourably placed than herself. She was forever telling Alex how she had left home in order to escape being suffocated by boredom and wealth, but she complained continually at having to

5

do without all the trappings of luxury which her brother had provided on his huge cattle station in the North. It was, though, partly because of this that Alex was rarely unsympathetic when Ruby grumbled, some of Ruby's problems, if not this particular one, seeming very similar to her own. From what Ruby said, her brother and Alex's mother might well be in the same league when it came to arrogantly managing the lives of others!

Alex often found herself reflecting with surprise at the strange way in which a mischievous fate had brought Ruby and herself together—two girls with very little in common. To leave home, was something the strong-willed Ruby had apparently been fighting to do for most of her life, while for Alex the desire to escape had only arisen a year ago, since she had left school.

Alex's parents had come to Australia when Alex was small. Her memories now of England were vague. Her father, a biochemist, worked on agricultural research near Sydney, in New South Wales. He had decided that Australia offered good opportunities for both himself and his son and daughter. His wife hadn't been so keen to emigrate. She was a snob and considered England offered opportunities of a different kind. Having better connections than her husband she had foreseen few difficulties in getting her children well settled. She had married for love, the only time in her life that she had allowed anything to get in the way of her better judgement, and privately regretted it ever since. She was determined neither Alex or her brother should make the same mistake. For them there should be better things than having to struggle along on what might seem a good salary to others, but represented a mere pittance to her. She shuddered to think how she could have managed without her own private income.

After settling down reluctantly in Sydney, she had prepared eventually to make the most of things. During the next few years she had worked hard, in what she considered a curiously classless society, to make her presence felt. From her mother's point of view, Alex supposed this strategy had paid off. She had managed to find Alan, Alex's brother, a wife from out of a well known and respected family. This, which she counted as success, and for which she took the entire credit, had appeared to go to her head, and with even more ambition in her heart she turned to Alex. Alex, having just left school, must have the right clothes, go to the right places, be seen with all the right people. In vain did Alex plead that she didn't want this kind of life, that her father couldn't afford it, that her mother would only make a laughing stock of them all if she persisted.

For months Alex had split her energy between her office job and trying to outmanoeuvre her mother. It wasn't until one young man whom her mother produced became embarrassingly persistent that she appealed to her father.

'She's only doing it so I can find a rich husband—and a husband's the last thing I want, Daddy, especially a rich one.'

'I'm sure your mother always acts for the best,' Richard Latham, loyal to the last, protested feebly.

For once Alex hadn't respected her father's obvious attempts to avoid a distressing subject. 'Why don't you put your foot down, Daddy? I'm sure you could if you tried, and it would help me. I don't want to settle down for years yet, and when I do I want to choose my own husband.'

'Your mother thinks young Fisher has fallen for you.'

'I don't even know if I like him!'

'Good connections there, mind you.'

Despairingly, Alex had stared at him, realising she must fight her own battles. Weeks later, though, when she was almost exhausted from the combined efforts of her mother and Don Fisher, something happened which convinced Alex that the gods hadn't deserted her altogether.

Help came in the form of an urgent message from England. Enid Latham's mother had been taken ill and was asking for her daughter. Mrs Latham had to go. During the first weeks she was gone, Alex did a lot of thinking and decided she would look for work elsewhere. She had been surprised and rather touched when her father had offered to help, ashamed that she had written him off as being completely under her mother's thumb.

'If it's any good to you, I know of a vacancy in a pastoral office in Melbourne, which isn't so very far away. At least,' he had given a rueful smile, 'it's far enough to enable you to avoid most of the social functions you don't care for but not too far to cause your mother and me undue worry.'

'A pastoral office?' she had queried.

'Well, it's only a suggestion. You could always try it.'

Melbourne, the capital of the State of Victoria. Yes, she quite liked the idea. 'Where would I stay, though?' she asked.

'You'd better go to a small hotel until you have time to have a look around. Your colleagues will probably be able to help you, once you get to know them.'

It had been easier than she had ever thought it would be. She had an interview and the job was hers. The vacancy had been left by an older woman who had unexpectedly married and gone to live in Western Australia. Her departure also left a vacancy in the flat which she had shared with another girl.

Ruby Marshall had scarcely glanced at Alex before telling her she was welcome to move in, providing she agreed to do most of the housework. As she had named a rent which was ridiculously low, Alex felt she would be crazy to refuse. What, after all, were a few dirty dishes? Who Ruby Marshall was, apart from being a fellow worker who was treated with great respect by the boss, didn't worry her unduly. It wasn't until after she saw the flat that she began to wonder, but such doubts had easily been forgotten as she strove to adjust to her new life.

Enid Latham, recently returned from England, had naturally nearly thrown a fit when she had discovered that during her absence her daughter had flown, but, other than making frequent phone calls, she hadn't done anything yet about dragging Alex back home. For this Alex suspected she had her father to thank, as well as a friend of her mother's, who had been brought out on a visit and was being energetically shown the sights of Sydney.

Alex was particularly relieved that her mother wasn't about to descend on her, as Ruby Marshall, while quite pleasant to live with, did practically nothing about the flat. Alex was kept so busy after work she didn't think she could have spared the time to entertain her mother. She glanced enquiringly at Ruby now. Ruby, shod in her silver shoes, was wandering around as though she wasn't going anywhere.

'Won't your boy-friend be waiting?' asked Alex.

'I suppose he might be,' Ruby shrugged her silken shoulders. 'Why do you ask? Do you want rid of me?'

'Of course not,' Alex replied quickly. 'All I'm going to do is wash my hair. I have to do it often.'

Ruby flicked an indifferent eye over it. 'That's because you're so fair, I expect.'

Alex smiled, far too sensible to accept this as a compliment. Ruby never really saw anyone but herself, and Alex suspected she had been offered a place in the flat only because Ruby had decided she was a spineless little thing, too quiet to object if she was ordered about. So she had been, during her first days in Melbourne, Alex would have been the first to admit. She had been exhausted from months of trying to keep one step ahead of her mother. Of trying to play down her looks, which

she didn't consider nearly so striking as her mother
liked to make out, in order to discourage the stream of
young men which Enid seemed to have an amazing
talent for producing.

Last week, however, Alex had had her hair properly
cut and styled. It was still shoulder-length but was now
like thick, gleaming silk which moved beautifully when
she walked and suited her much better than the tightly
curled version her mother favoured. This style gave
Alex's long, slender neck and well balanced head an air
of delicate dignity. She had the look of a highly strung
fawn with her slender limbs and small waist and the
hint of wariness in her lovely blue eyes which, unfortunately, her mother had been largely responsible for putting there.

If Ruby hadn't paid much attention to her before, she
was certainly taking a good look at Alex now, and was
obviously rather startled by Alex's fresh young beauty.
'Why don't you go out with Martin James, from the
office?' she asked. 'He's always chasing you. It would
make a nice change.'

Ruby would never suggest Alex moved in the same
exclusive circles as she did. Alex hid a slight smile. 'I
don't think I'm interested in Martin, at least not
enough to go out with him. Does it matter how I spend
my spare time?'

'To me—no,' Ruby was always frank. 'I'll probably
be moving on soon, anyway. Quite frankly, I think I've
had just about enough of Melbourne. In some ways,'
she commented mysteriously, 'it's almost as bad as
home. After my holiday I might try Sydney for a while.'

Slowly Alex digested that. If Ruby moved on she
would be giving up the flat, which would mean she
would have to start hunting for a place of her own. And
she would never be able to afford a place like this.

'What will your brother say if you leave Melbourne?'
she asked unhappily.

'It's what he's going to say if I don't,' Ruby grumbled cryptically. 'The man I'm friendly with just now, for instance. I like him, but I know Chase wouldn't.'

'You can't possibly know until they meet, surely?' said Alex, suddenly sensing Ruby needed soothing. 'Why tell your brother? From what you've told me of him, he has too many other interests to worry over-much about what his sister's up to.'

'You don't know Chase. He even knows what his youngest, most unimportant employees are up to. A sister, an immediate member of his family, as far as he's concerned, is a piece of cake.'

'Well, don't let him eat you up.' Alex grinned, admiring Ruby's flair for expressing herself exactly. 'If you haven't the strength, and this man is important to you, use your wits. I'm sure you have plenty.'

Ruby accepted this as a compliment. She would never believe Alex would dare have a sly dig at her. She glanced at Alex tautly. 'Chase has arrogance as well as intelligence, my dear. My grandfather used to be the same. So is Aunt Harriet, but Chase is worse, I think, than either of them. He's just impossible to fight on his own grounds. Head on I wouldn't stand a chance.'

'Then do it behind his back.' Alex never stopped for a moment to consider that her advice might be rash. If she had done, the possibility of such power as Ruby implied being toppled by means such as she suggested was so remote as to remove any seriousness from it. What she had impulsively suggested was prompted more from a wish to comfort Ruby than any real desire to goad her to defy her brother. From experience she knew what it was like to be caught in the machinations of family ambitions, but it seemed incredible that a girl of Ruby Marshall's age and sophistication should even recognise a higher power.

'My dear child,' Ruby's tone rejected Alex's advice scornfully, 'no one ever gets the better of my brother.

Even escaping this far nearly killed me. Believe me it was a major victory, but a hollow one for all that. Normally, he would never have allowed it.'

This bordered a little too much on hysterical exaggeration to be wholly acceptable, yet Ruby had never looked as disturbed as she did now, not in all the weeks they had been together. What she said had a curious ring of truth, urging Alex to ask, 'Why did he let you go this time, then?'

'I'm not sure.' Ruby was blind to the doubt in Alex's eyes. 'Perhaps he saw I was driven. He would like me to encourage a neighbour of ours. He seems to think a girl's chances of marriage don't improve after twenty-six, but I have my own ideas in that direction. As he is soon to discover!' she finished waspishly.

Alex said quietly, 'Maybe your brother's not as set on this as you believe. If he was then why should he have agreed to your living here?'

'I've told you, I'm not sure!' Ruby snapped impatiently. 'Perhaps he thought he could keep an eye on me here just as well as at home. There has to be a reason, but I haven't tried too hard to find it. I'm just taking what's offered without asking too many questions.'

'But you said he'll know everything you're doing?'

'So he might,' Ruby shrugged, 'but I haven't seen him for weeks. I have reason to believe he's well occupied on the other side of the globe, which can be the only explanation.'

'Occupied?' queried Alex.

'An attractive brunette, my dear, who'll only say no long enough to make it worth her while.'

Ruby's cynicism struck Alex as regrettable. It also shocked her slightly. Chase Marshall did, too. Much more so. A kind of horrified fascination with the Marshall family caught her in a curious grip, forcing her to query with wide-eyed incredulity, 'Does your brother always allow his girl-friends to drive him to such lengths?'

'Not always, and he was going to America, anyway,' Ruby admitted reluctantly. 'He doesn't usually have to exert himself in the least to get his own way. Women seem to make a habit of falling for his looks and his money, but he's generally less than impressed.'

'Always?'

Again Ruby shrugged. 'Oh, some last a few months. His affairs are usually brief. He seems to lose interest very easily. That's probably why he's never married.'

Alex smiled maliciously, not caring for the picture she saw. 'Perhaps someone's refused him?'

Ruby shook her head. 'None of us ever recall him betraying even a flicker of anxiety, let alone a broken heart. And we would have known.'

'Does it have to show?'

'Chase wouldn't allow it.' Ruby's absolute conviction amazed Alex. 'The lady wouldn't stand a chance. He'd have it all cut and dried, she wouldn't have a leg to stand on!' With a sigh, she rose to her feet. 'You must allow me to know my own brother, Alex, especially as you've never even met him.'

This wasn't likely. And more likely, if she ever did, he wouldn't so much as notice her. The kind of man Chase Marshall was put him well beyond the experience of girls like herself. Convinced of this, Alex observed dryly, 'You don't show your brother in a very pretty light, Ruby. You don't make him sound a very nice person at all.'

'He isn't,' yet there was an unconscious pride in Ruby's voice. 'I don't think there are many men like him, but he can be lethal when thwarted.'

'Can't we all?'

'You may laugh, Alex,' Ruby tied a scarf over her beautifully waved hair to protect it from the wind that was rising. 'It's not exactly a joke for me, though. You can't imagine what it's like, having to fight continually against being married off.'

How could she reply to this without betraying her

own story? Alex stared at Ruby unhappily. Loyalty for her mother made such a confession impossible, whereas Ruby appeared to have no such scruples. Although, to give Ruby her due, this was the first time she had been so frank about her family.

'I mightn't mind so much,' she hedged weakly, 'if I really liked the man.'

'Oh, Henry's all right,' Ruby admitted, 'but he's so unexciting. Marriage to him would mean I'd merely be exchanging one boring old station for another. You've no idea how lonely life can be in the Outback, unless you like that kind of thing. I . . .'

The doorbell rang and Ruby departed, breaking off abruptly in mid-sentence, almost as if she was relieved at the interruption. As if suddenly she feared she had said too much. 'See you,' she frowned, on her way out.

Once she had gone, Alex got down to the serious business of washing her hair. Contrary to what she had told Ruby, it wasn't really in need of a wash, but once she had finished her usual tasks around the flat an odd restlessness wouldn't let her sit still. Ruby's outpourings had unsettled her, even while she knew Ruby would regret them before morning. Ruby was a strange girl, an odd mixture of personalities. She certainly seemed to have a problem, regarding her brother, but Alex couldn't see how she could help her. Underneath, she had a sneaking feeling that Ruby might be more than able to help herself.

She had just finished drying and combing her hair, impressed by a new rinse she had found, when the doorbell rang again. Had Ruby forgotten something? Not an unusual occurrence. Or it might be one of her other young men? Sometimes she made dates and forgot about them, leaving to Alex the thankless task of having to soothe ruffled feelings.

Striving hurriedly to make herself appear respectable, Alex drew the sash of her satin robe tighter as she ran to the door, not realising how this emphasised the full, taut breasts above her narrow waist. Alex was all slenderness and refinement, but nature had been more generous to her than most in this respect.

A faint smile on her lips faded as she opened the door to a complete stranger. He was over six foot, with broad shoulders, but was lean and tough-looking rather than heavy. His hair was thick and dark, his features striking with a straight nose and deeply cleft chin. His eyes, a grey that seemed to deepen and then lighten as he glanced at her, were set under arrogant brows. Yet the sense of power that immediately struck her was more of personality. Or was it his mouth? Crazily her pondering thoughts veered. Never had she seen a mouth so strong-looking and wilful. Even the white teeth, bared in a conventional smile, looked capable of doing much more than what they were originally intended for. With a visible shudder she quite irrationally felt them biting into her soft skin and shrank back.

'Good evening,' she stammered, attempting to find enough breath to suggest he had the wrong address. Whatever would a man like this be doing here?

Returning her greeting dryly, he continued to study her as closely as she had him. If he approved of her extremely slender frame, the fact that the top of her head barely reached his shoulder, he gave no indication. His voice was the only pleasant thing about him, Alex decided, but she was shaken when he asked coolly, 'Am I right in thinking a Miss Marshall lives here? Miss Ruby Marshall, my sister?'

She might have known! Her cheeks colouring faintly, Alex almost exclaimed, 'Why, we've just been talking about you!' Fortunately she didn't. With a man like this one wouldn't indulge in such run-of-the-mill remarks.

'I—you'd better come in, Mr—er—Marshall,' she choked. 'Ruby's out.' That didn't sound right and the colour in her cheeks deepened in a way she could see attracted his attention. 'I——' she was mortified to hear herself stammering again, like a schoolgirl, 'perhaps you would rather come back when she's in?'

'Naturally I will.' He walked past her, a flicker of amusement on his face at her obvious consternation. 'Are you hiding something in here you don't want me to see? A man, maybe?'

Quickly Alex closed the door, blessing a devious fate for sending him at this particular hour. 'If I had a man here, Mr Marshall, there would be no need to hide him. Oh!' Suddenly comprehending, she glared with rage as he stared at her robe, a scrap of material against which her rounded curves pushed almost suggestively. Incredibly it seemed as though her body was responding blindly to a complete stranger. Thank goodness her mind still retained some degree of sanity. 'You don't imagine,' she spluttered, 'that I've got someone in my bedroom?'

'I'll soon find out!' Ignoring her furious expression, he strode over the small hall to fling open bedroom doors. 'Ruby's room—yours?' As she nodded in helpless agreement, he cruised on, a human torpedo and just about as devastating. 'The kitchen, the bathroom and the lounge. Well, unless your boy-friend's hiding on the roof, you don't have one. Not here, anyway.'

'Mr Marshall!' Feeling about to burst with an uncontrollable force of temper, Alex glared at him. 'I happen to share this flat with your sister, not half a dozen men. She lets me stay for very little, and I'm grateful, but that doesn't mean I have to put up with insults from her family!'

Not the least disturbed by her anger, he said curtly, 'I haven't finished yet. You may not care for the way I go about things, but I certainly have a right to know what's going on! As I pay for the flat so I believe I have every right to ask questions.' He paused, his eyes glinting, 'I don't know what arrangements you and Ruby have between you, but I do know that last time I was here she was sharing with a middle-aged woman. Something I personally arranged, as I happen to feel responsible for my sister. Maybe you can tell me where this other lady has gone?'

'My name is Latham,' Alex gasped, shaking, never having been spoken to in such a manner before. She could well believe Ruby's brother was everything Ruby said he was! 'You must mean Lilian Beck, who left before I came?'

'Exactly.'

How Alex hated the feeling that he was superbly if insufferably in control of the situation, while she, because she wasn't sure what Ruby would wish her to say, was floundering. 'I was told that Miss Beck met and married someone within a week, and has gone to live in Western Australia, not far from Perth.'

'A whirlwind romance?'

The cynicism in his voice came over clearly. Alex retorted, 'You obviously don't believe in such a thing.'

'No way,' he agreed crisply, adding, if a little less savagely, 'Why wasn't I informed?'

'I've no idea.' Alex's smile was deliberately provocative, meant to annoy. 'Do you have to be told everything, Mr Marshall? I don't think Ruby knew where you were.'

'She knows how to get in touch, and I'll have something to say to Miss Beck if we meet again. You're far too young for the job I entrusted to her—and Ruby must know it.'

Swiftly, Alex spoke. 'I'm not quite sure what you have in mind, but I'm nineteen.'

'Really?' His frosty grey eyes sparkled, almost grazing the still slightly babyish fulness of her satiny cheeks. 'Am I supposed to be impressed?'

He was eleven years older than Ruby, so he wouldn't be. If what he said was true then he must be entitled to lay down the law, but it didn't make her like him any better. Alex was surprised at the weight of her dislike, even allowing for his insults. It was making her feel quite violent inside, like a kettle boiling with no outlet for the steam. A little more and she might explode! Unable to trust herself, she made no reply to his last taunt, merely shook her pale golden head soberly.

He was much cooler than she was when he spoke again. 'Have you any idea when Ruby is due back?'

'Er—she's never very late.'

The only response to this being a raised eyebrow, Alex wondered why he had bothered to ask. 'It might be better if you saw her tomorrow.' Surely he didn't intend waiting tonight? How would she entertain him? Her heart beat fast at the prospect. They both knew the dawn might beat Ruby in.

'Tomorrow won't do. I'll be gone then and I have things to say.' Chase Marshall paused speculatively, as though dwelling on a matter which angered him. His jaw tightened as his eyes hardened. 'Things that won't keep,' he snapped.

If he paid the rent, what could she do? 'Then make yourself at home,' she invited coldly.

He said, softly menacing, 'There's nothing very welcoming in your voice, Miss Latham. You could try making it a little warmer.'

Again she smiled sweetly. 'I'm sure you won't be losing any sleep over that, Mr Marshall. Why not forget I exist? After all, it's Ruby you want to see.'

'Have you a drink?' he asked abruptly, adding with hard mockery, 'I'll need something, I'm thinking.'

'Because of me?'

'Only your looks are saving you,' he muttered, 'from going over my knee. When you learn to smile at a man instead of provoking him with your tongue, you might get somewhere.'

While not quite sure what he meant, Alex had the

grace to feel ashamed, unable to say why he had the ability to make her act completely out of character. There was no reason why they shouldn't talk like polite strangers. No reason she could think of why she should be feeling so intensely antagonistic.

'I'm sorry, I'll get you a drink.' Walking towards it rather blindly, she groped in the cupboard where Ruby kept it.

Before she could do anything more, Chase was by her side, taking charge, running his eyes expertly over the various bottles. Removing a full bottle of whisky, he broke the seal. As he did so, his glance swivelled thoughtfully over Alex. 'Go and get some clothes on and I'll take you out to dinner. It might be easier on us both than staying here.'

Did he always talk in riddles? she wondered. Why was she not arguing? She did protest, but it wasn't the outright refusal she intended making. 'I can easily make you something here. There's no need——'

'I quite agree, but I'm not acting out of charity or because you look as if you could do with a good square meal. I'm hungry and I feel like going out.'

'You don't have to take me, though.'

Chase ignored this, helping himself to more whisky, as though her contrariness was directly responsible for driving him to drink. He stared at her over the top of his glass and somehow she knew better than to go on opposing him.

As she left him to dress Alex could feel herself trembling. The shaded blue silk would do very well. It was decorous, which might prove to Chase Marshall that she wasn't a girl to indulge frequently in this kind of outing with strangers. Behaviour and dress might express some things better than words. He should learn that the green satin dressing gown, over which he had cast several considering glances, was just not her.

Yet, after she was ready, she wondered why the high

rolled collar of the demure little dress failed to please her this evening. Frowning, she viewed herself in the mirror, without finding the answer. Perhaps the neckline could have been a little lower without offending anyone. Her mother had been with her when she had purchased it and she had never questioned her mother's impeccable good taste before. To do so now made Alex feel even guiltier than she had when she had fled from Sydney.

Of course she had never met a man like Chase Marshall before. She felt nervous even to think of him. There were qualities in him of power and discipline, enough to make a girl far older than Alex take fright. Ruby had been right about the arrogance. It stood out a mile. It made the prospect of dining with him something to be regarded with sheer apprehension.

He spoke very little until they were seated in a restaurant in South Yarra, one which Alex had heard was one of the best in Melbourne. It was discreet and comfortable without being ostentatious, and the food was good. Chase Marshall appeared to be well known. She noticed how the waiters appeared to spring to life when they walked in, and how they were at his side immediately, whenever he flicked his finger.

His swift appraisal of her had held a certain hint of admiration, as she came out of her bedroom wearing a creamy fur cape around her shoulders. What had he expected? she wondered.

After he had ordered he turned to her again, startling her completely when he said, 'You're young, very innocent, I imagine. Totally unsuitable for the position you're now occupying.' Once more his eyes went closely over her face. 'You look about seventeen.'

Because she didn't care to be summed up and condemned so disparagingly, Alex countered with a matching attempt at frankness, 'If I do look two years younger than I actually am, I don't think I could say the same for you.' Deliberately, although it took some doing, she concentrated her eyes on the lines that carved his hard handsome face, the deep ones on his broad intelligent forehead, those running from his nose to the sides of his sensuous mouth. 'You look older.'

'Which suggests you know exactly how old I am?'

She fancied, with satisfaction, his cool tones hid some slight annoyance, perhaps a little male vanity. 'Your sister has mentioned you occasionally, Mr Marshall. Thirty-six—or is it seven—isn't so very old.'

She might have been mistaken about the glint of anger, for he merely shrugged, very sure, apparently, of his own worth. 'My age hasn't proved a handicap yet, Miss Latham. But then I'm not a woman. You're nineteen, then. Almost twenty?'

'No. I'm just past my birthday.'

'My God!' It was softly but emphatically spoken and white teeth snapped. 'Why should Ruby imagine I would approve of a child like you as a chaperone?'

Alex's gentian blue eyes widened. 'Do you have to, Mr Marshall? And does she really need a chaperone?'

'Naturally.' He appeared astonished that she should question this. 'Miss Beck was ideally suitable, but you certainly aren't.'

As far as chaperones went, he must be right, for Alex had never seen herself in such a role before. Ruby had never so much as suggested it when she had asked Alex to share the flat. Chase Marshall's disapproval, however, seemed to point at other things besides age.

'While I realise your opinion of my capabilities doesn't amount to much,' she replied sharply, 'haven't you forgotten your sister's twenty-six? Surely old enough to make even the suggestion of a chaperone sound ridiculous?'

His jaw tightened impatiently. He obviously wasn't used to having his motives questioned. 'It wasn't in the conventional sense.'

'Oh, I see. You mean Miss Beck was supposed to spy and report?'

'If you like.' He didn't turn a hair.

'I think that's despicable!'

'I'd be careful what you say, Miss Latham, if I were you,' his grey eyes hardened coldly. 'I can see you're a girl who's never learnt to think before she speaks, but allow me to know my own sister, and to know what's best for her. She has certain commitments at home that I won't allow her to wriggle out of.'

Suddenly Alex wondered why she was bothering. Indifferently she shrugged. 'Well, I suppose you'll soon be seeing your sister and getting it all sorted out. It's really none of my business.'

'Who has she gone out with tonight?'

Alex sighed, giving up, Chase Marshall never would—he was that kind of man. She might only exhaust herself if she continued fighting him. 'A man whom I believe she's known for some time.' For Ruby's sake she did her best to make it sound a very proper friendship. 'I've met him, he's called Alexander Brown. It's rather strange that he should have the same Christian name as me, only mine's the feminine version.'

'You're known as——?'

'Alex.'

'I see,' he smiled tightly. 'This gets more interesting. Do you know if she's very fond of this man?'

Alex looked at him, remembering what Ruby had said about Chase wanting to get her married off. She must be careful—perhaps she had already said too much. 'I'm not sure how she feels about him,' she replied uncomfortably. 'I just know that she likes him.'

CHAPTER TWO

WHEN Chase Marshall spoke again, Alex heard the insistence in his voice with a small qualm of fear. 'This could be serious?'

'Look, Mr Marshall,' she exclaimed, 'I have no idea. I've met Mr Brown—he seems very nice and Ruby goes out with him, but more than that I can't tell you. And I do think we should talk of something else.'

'We could do,' he agreed, but with a glitter in his eyes, for he was clearly used to dictating the conversation. Yet, to Alex's surprise, he was apparently as willing as she was to drop the subject. Her relief was short-lived, however, when he began concentrating on herself. Double-checking, she supposed, attempting to avoid anything more than the most casual answers.

'Have you lived in Australia long, Miss Latham?' When she glanced at him enquiringly, he smiled sardonically. 'A slight difference in tone always gives people away.'

'Since I was ten,' she admitted.

'And you're still very much an English rose.' His grey eyes concentrated on each of her features as he alluded to them. 'Hair the colour of English primroses in the soft spring rain, creamy skin, beautifully tinted with pink. Only your eyes are a deeper blue than your average English skies, and I believe I should have said a rosebud, rather than a rose?'

His voice was too dry to be complimentary, so she declined to thank him. The creamy soufflé she was eating was delicious and she gave it her whole attention. She knew what he was hinting at, but refused to rise to the bait. Whether she was innocent or not was none of his business, and she would be no match for his expertise, no matter what field he decided to play in. Her only refuge lay in silence.

Unperturbed by it, he continued idly, 'Why aren't you still living at home with your parents?'

'Because they happen to live in Sydney.'

'Really? I wonder they dared let you out of their sight.'

'Not everyone's that possessive, Mr Marshall,' she retorted, then went white when she thought of her mother.

His eyes narrowed, as if he would like to find out what bothered her. 'You'll be telling me next that women don't care for being protected, looked after!'

'I wouldn't dare to presume to tell you anything, Mr Marshall. You obviously have a mind of your own.' Alex's chin set at a very delicate angle. 'The modern woman . . .'

He put in ruthlessly, as she drew a reviving little breath, 'I hardly think that applies to you, Alex, on either count.'

Softly she blazed back at him, unable to understand why she should feel mortally wounded, 'I may not be a woman yet, but I'm not sure that I'm missing much—that I want to be. I've made up my mind . . .'

'If I had time I could soon change it for you.'

Unevenly her pulse jerked, began racing, even as she recognised him as insufferable—sophisticated, stamped with his own self-confident authority. One day she hoped some woman would bring him low. 'I must just be grateful you haven't time for me, then,' she said sweetly.

'You'd be very easy to make time for, Alex Latham.' He picked up his glass and raised it to her, his eyes mocking, 'If you were a little older I might seriously consider it.'

She smiled, watching his eyes turn to silver. The smile

on her softly curved lips was more wistful than she knew. 'I won't always be nineteen.'

'The gap won't close, though.'

'The one of age? No, it won't. I suppose girls of my age bore you.'

'Only when they talk as you do.' His eyes stayed on her tremulous mouth before moving deliberately to meet hers. 'Tell me,' he probed gently, 'what does your father do for a living?'

'He's a biochemist. He works for a firm in Sydney.' She gave the name and he nodded.

'I know it. How long since you began working in Melbourne?'

Without giving very much away, she told him, then courageously asked what his plans were. 'Ruby says you don't spend a lot of time at home.'

'I run a company, Alex, not just one station. If I did just that, life would be a whole lot simpler, but for Ruby and the other members of my family not nearly so well padded. Did she tell you that, I wonder?'

'Is wealth all that important?'

'To many people it's still the most important thing there is,' he said dryly.

Again Alex thought of her mother. Carefully she said, 'Ruby told me you like being at the station.'

'It's called Coolabra,' he enlightened her, 'and I love it. I have a passion for it that my sister doesn't share. The only thing she enjoys is the luxury it provides.'

'But it couldn't do that on its own.'

'I hardly think so.'

He stared at her broodingly, his eyes never leaving her, while apparently his mind pursued other things. It was as though he had two separate trains of thought on which he concentrated with equal absorption, his beloved cattle station and his business interests away from it. It must be purely incidental, Alex felt, that for some reason she couldn't fathom, she was receiving more than her share of his reluctant attention. No woman, she fancied, would absorb him completely. That day might never come!

Later he took her back to the flat, through the dark reflecting lights of the city. He drove a long luxurious car which was obviously his own, but when she asked him if he had had a long drive getting to Melbourne, he smiled.

'I travel by air. It's quicker and less wearing. I have apartments both here and in Sydney.'

She didn't ask whereabouts in Sydney, but she was still digesting this as they reached the flat. Evidently his business commitments must force him to spend some time in both places, but both cities were big, there would be no likelihood of running into him when she went home.

Thinking it might help to ease a sudden, inexplicable tension between them, she suggested coffee while they waited for Ruby. Chase nodded, but when she came back with it he was drinking whisky again. He drank as though he needed it, and she wondered why.

Passing his coffee, she was unaware of the reproving look in her eyes which had his mouth twisting wryly as he accepted his cup and helped himself to sugar. While he drank it he regarded her intently, as he had done while they were out, and Alex wished he wouldn't. It was almost as if she presented a conundrum he didn't quite know how to solve. She couldn't recall ever being scrutinised so closely before by anyone and her heart began reacting strangely. It raced in her breast and she turned from him to hide her agitation.

A sigh of relief escaped her stiff lips when Ruby came home early. Murmuring a hurried goodnight, she turned a blind eye to Ruby's startled consternation. Clearly she wasn't pleased to see her brother.

As Alex went into her bedroom she heard Ruby say she was going to make herself a cup of tea. She actually followed Alex from the lounge to go to the kitchen. Chase Marshall must have followed his sister, for she could hear them talking. Because the walls were so thin, Alex could make out what they were saying to each other. It didn't appear to occur to either of them to lower their voices.

The kitchenette, next to Alex's bedroom, was small. Chase hadn't gone right inside. He would be lounging against the doorpost, as many of Ruby's male friends did. His voice came, terse with impatience. 'Where the hell have you been, Ruby?'

'Out.' There came the sound of the kettle being filled, then Ruby adding impertinently, 'I can see something's upset you. What exactly are you complaining about?'

'Just having to kick my heels for hours, being bored stiff!'

Ruby's hoot of laughter was bitchy. 'Didn't you find young Alex entertaining?'

'No, I did not!'

Alex felt her face go slowly cold. Glancing in the mirror before diving to cover her head with a pillow, she saw she had gone quite white. Chase Marshall had affected her oddly, but somehow she had liked him. Under all her surging uncertainty something inside her had seemed to reach out to him, and she had felt he liked her, too. And all the time he had been bored! How stupid she had been to imagine it could be otherwise. Yet, if he had been fed up, couldn't he have kept it to himself? Did he have to tell Ruby? Tears stung Alex's eyes and she hated him. Never again would she trust a man!

Suffocating, she had to come up for air. They were still talking, Chase's voice hard. 'You wrote to Isobel Berry and told her you were going on holiday with someone called Alex.'

'You've just had her out to dinner.'

'But she isn't the Alex you meant. She isn't even due

a holiday yet—I asked her. You've been out tonight with a man called Alexander. Alex, I suppose, for short.'

'Who told you?'

'Miss Latham.'

'Oh, the little fool!'

'I think you're the fool, my dear. Your friend Isobel's been on the transceiver and it's all over the North. Henry's heard and he's furious.'

'Isobel Berry?' Ruby screamed. 'I trusted her!'

'I can't think why.' Chase Marshall sounded extremely dry. 'You know she's been chasing Henry for years.'

'But she's my best friend!'

'Is she?' again the extreme dryness.

'I'm not engaged to Henry,' protested Ruby.

'Then you'd better make up your mind or you might not get another chance.' Chase paused, then asked silkily, 'If you intended going on holiday with Alex Latham, why doesn't she know about it?'

'Because I haven't told her yet.'

'Right,' Chase's voice was crisp, 'you can tell her in the morning, no need to wake her up tonight. And when she asks where she's going, you can tell her to Coolabra. I'll pick you both up at Alice Springs.'

'I'm not coming home!'

'You'd better decide to. All the Territory believes you're going to the Barrier Reef with a man, so you'd better be prepared to bring Miss Latham along to convince people—Henry particularly—that Alex is a girl. It's either this or goodbye to Henry. And if that's finished, so are you. I've stood all I'm going to stand for the time being.'

Ruby's voice sounded nervous, but she jeered, 'How will you stand having Alex Latham around? She's clearly not your type.'

'No, she isn't, but I won't be there more than a day

or two. Just long enough to see you settled in. I've spent enough time already.'

Alex didn't go to sleep, not even when Ruby and her brother went to the lounge and she couldn't hear them distinctly any more. Chase didn't stay much longer, but while he did he appeared to be the one who was now doing all the talking. Ruby was apparently being suitably chastised.

She hadn't expected to see Ruby until the next morning, so she was surprised when, after Chase had gone, Ruby burst into the bedroom. Alex, pretending she had been asleep, opened wary eyes and waited.

Sullenly, Ruby cried, 'Why had you to go telling Chase about Alexander?'

'He asked, and I didn't think it was a secret.'

Ruby stared down at her impatiently. 'Now I have to spend my holiday at Coolabra. Not only that, he wants you there, too.'

'Me?' Alex managed to look completely startled. 'Why me?'

'Because I was stupid enough to confide in a friend that I was going on holiday with someone called Alex. Now Chase wants you at Coolabra to convince people that Alex is really and truly a girl.'

'Were you really serious about going on holiday with Alexander?'

'I was thinking about it,' said Ruby lightly. 'Anyway, Henry Brett, he's the neighbour I was telling you about, the one Chase wants me to marry, has heard and he's furious!'

Suddenly Alex had a sneaking suspicion that Ruby rather liked the idea of Henry being furious. 'Do you love this neighbour?' she asked, brushing back her tumbled hair, as if to give Ruby her whole attention.

Ruby frowned, some of her self-confidence leaving her. 'Don't you see, that's what I've been trying to find out. Why I'm going out with other men. Chase just won't give me time.'

Alex smiled grimly, her heart still sore from Chase Marshall's insults. 'Well, I'm afraid I won't be going with you. For one thing, I haven't been with the firm long enough to ask for a holiday. I'm not entitled to one yet, and if I were I wouldn't be spending it with you. I'm not being rude,' she added hastily, 'but I know you wouldn't want me, and your brother has no authority to order me around.'

At six the next morning, Alex woke to hear someone talking. This being unusual, at this hour of the day in the flat, she jumped out of bed to investigate, and was astonished to find it was Ruby on the telephone. Drawing back, before Ruby realised she was there, she found herself once again guilty of eavesdropping.

Ruby spoke in a low voice. 'She won't agree, Chase. I'll try again when she wakes up, but I'm sure she won't change her mind.'

A pause, then, 'Yes, I know you haven't met a woman yet who couldn't be persuaded to change her mind, but I'm not a man. I've never had to use my charm on a woman—I wouldn't know where to begin!'

Another impatient pause. 'Well, you're certainly welcome to try. Poor girl, I doubt if she'll stand a chance. I thought you were going straight to Sydney?'

A minute later: 'Yes, I can be out by ten. I'll leave the coast clear. Goodbye, Chase.'

Alex was in bed with her eyes closed when Ruby silently opened her door to see if she was still sleeping. Quietly the older girl withdrew, leaving Alex seething. So Chase Marshall thought he had only to lift a little finger and she would agree to do as he asked! Well, he was going to have to think again, because she wouldn't change her mind about going to Coolabra. It wasn't just that he had confessed unashamedly to being bored stiff by her company, or his cool assumption that he had only to beckon and she would come running; it was something else, something she hadn't got figured out yet, that was warning her to keep away from Chase Marshall for her own peace of mind.

She was angry yet terribly shaken, fraught by emotions she didn't understand, that flowed through her in a deeply disturbing stream. It was like being attacked by an unseen, unknown enemy, but while she came to the conclusion that Chase Marshall must have triggered something off, she couldn't believe that such feelings were because of him. It must simply be some slight revival of the reactions she had known when she had first left her home to come to Melbourne. Something she had thought she had got over nicely.

Having braced herself against further persuasion by Ruby, she was surprised when the girl departed, without saying a word, at about nine-thirty to keep her usual Saturday morning appointment with her hairdresser. It could have been, Alex decided, that Ruby felt she might only make things worse. On the other hand, now that she had perhaps had time to think things over, she might not be as keen as her brother to have Alex at Coolabra.

Alex didn't dress. If Chase Marshall expected to surprise her she would let him believe she was surprised. At first she thought of having a showdown straight away, but dismissing this as too melodramatic, she settled for telling him coolly that she couldn't be persuaded to change her mind about visiting his cattle station. For an excuse she would simply say she didn't want to go there.

Then she wavered. Why make it so clean and simple? Didn't he deserve to suffer, if only a few wasted hours? Why not string the great man along, let him believe she was really as gullible as he thought? She had had an expensive dinner out of him—why not lunch? If she was very clever and used her wits, as some of the girls in the office did to their advantage, she might get even more out of him—which would make the watching of his face when she eventually turned him down even more pleasurable!

When the doorbell rang her heart was beating heavily. It struck her that Chase must want this match between his neighbour and Ruby very much to be putting himself out as he was doing. Why else would he be going to such lengths to convince this Henry Brett that Ruby wasn't going on holiday with another man? He had even postponed his original plans to leave Melbourne early today in order to talk to a girl who, he had confessed quite openly, didn't give him any pleasure to be with.

On opening the door to Chase Marshall, Alex had to admit she might find very few men like him. Dressed in a pair of casual pants and light jacket, he still had an aura of wealth and power, an authority that almost altered her breathing as she wondered how she even dared think of fighting him. She wasn't aware how her face was revealing character traits of her own. One moment she looked cool and self-confident, the next, anxious and shy.

'Oh!' She contrived to appear startled, relieved that he would mistake the guilty flush on her cheeks for confusion. 'I didn't expect to see you back, Mr Marshall. I'm afraid Ruby's out, having her hair done.'

'I changed my mind about leaving this morning,' he smiled charmingly, with little respect for Alex's heart, 'and it's not Ruby I've come to see.'

'Which only leaves me.' Whimsically, Alex tried to give the impression of amused sophistication as he deftly manoeuvred himself inside and closed the door.

'Yes,' he didn't beat about the bush, 'that only leaves you.' He hesitated, his eyes flicking over her tight jeans and tighter tee-shirt. 'I take it you don't have a similar appointment this morning?'

'I do my own hair.'

'It's quite charming.' He sounded as if he meant it. 'Last night I admired the colour. This morning,' he put out a hand and touched it gently, 'in the sunshine, it's even more beautiful.'

Sharply Alex withdrew her head, stopping short of an actual jerk. She wanted to say, 'Last night you were bored stiff; the colour of my hair made no difference to your real feelings.' Instead she lowered her eyes, not altogether deliberately, away from his suddenly intent gaze. 'Thank you,' she murmured distantly.

Again he hesitated. Alex was sure he never did as a rule, which must be why his voice sounded terse. 'I believe you turned down the invitation Ruby gave you to visit Coolabra?'

Not it was Alex's turn to hesitate. Not having expected him to bring up the subject so quickly, she was unprepared. Instinct guided her to answer, as though overwhelmed, 'It's quite a big step, Mr Marshall.'

Expecting to be bombarded with immediate arguments as to why she should acquiesce at once, she was startled when he said, 'I have to go to Geelong. It's only fifty miles or so. How about coming with me and I'll tell you something of Coolabra on the way? Come as you are, if you like. We can always buy some food and have a picnic lunch on the beach.'

Alex felt like laughing. They must both be playing the same waiting game if with different goals in view. Again it struck her that Chase must be very keen to get his sister's affairs settled, if he was willing to endure being bored again by Alex Latham. As for herself, it was exactly what she had been angling after—wasn't it?

Almost she decided to take him at his word and go as she was. Until she remembered her chosen role. He must soon find out that lunch was going to cost him much more than a few sandwiches and a bottle of Coke! Smiling sweetly, she shook her head, begging him to wait while she changed.

In her bedroom she paused. Why not begin right away? She could keep him waiting at least half an hour. If he didn't like it—and she suspected he wouldn't be used to it—he could always go!

He didn't. He was still there when she returned in a light dress, which had only taken her moments to change into. He was lounging in the largest chair, drinking tea and reading yesterday's newspaper.

'Charming,' he commented, his eyes going lazily over her. 'Well worth waiting for.'

He was letting her know he knew. She could tell by the glint in his eye, behind the laziness. 'I hope I haven't been too long?' It was well over half an hour since she had left him.

'It doesn't matter,' suavely he heaved himself upright, 'a little patience and I usually get what I want in the end.'

Wondering why she persisted, Alex was unable to resist pointing out concisely, 'That's a different kind of waiting, though.'

'Possibly,' he conceded her victory just so far.

'And you haven't been bored stiff?' She would liked to have stressed those last two words, but her courage failed her.

'No,' he threw her a suddenly sharp glance, which unfortunately only confirmed that she had heard him aright the night before, yet his tongue was smooth as he relaxed and continued, 'As you can see, I've made myself at home. If it soothes your conscience, I quite enjoyed making myself a cup of tea and reading the newspaper. An odd item caught my eye that I hadn't known about.'

He was a fine one to be talking about anyone's conscience! Alex thought angrily, as they left the flat. His car was outside and just as comfortable this morning, she felt her body slither sensuously against the soft leather seat. She settled uneasily as Chase drove swiftly but carefully through the light industrial areas on the west of the city to reach the Princes Highway. Geelong, on the western shores of Port Philip Bay, was the gateway to the western district of Victoria and most of the district between Melbourne and it was built up. Beyond Altona lay the Air Force base at Laverton, where they joined the main highway and went on to the market town of Werribee, an area of dairy farming and vegetable growing. There was also a large metropolitan farm, Chase told her, with more head of cattle than many of the huge stations in northern Australia.

Alex, who had never been this far before, found she was listening keenly to everything he told her. She hadn't intended enjoying herself at all, but he made such an excellent guide she found it difficult not to. He took a great interest in everything around him. He would, she acknowledged to herself reluctantly, realising this would be half the secret of his astonishing vitality.

Geelong was a busy port that served the local industries and sent out around twenty-five per cent of Australia's wheat exports. It also had major annual wool sales, which Chase said he usually attended, but most of the wool went out from Melbourne. Alex waited in the car while he disappeared into a huge office block. He wasn't gone long and she was surprised to find how pleased she was to see him back.

'Missed me?' he smiled, his manner not too familiar.

Shaking her head, she denied it shamelessly. 'Did you expect me to? We haven't known each other all that long.'

'No, we haven't, have we?' he agreed, the beginnings of a doubtful frown disappearing.

For a second she felt startled. She could only have imagined he was taking comfort from the thought. She had sensed briefly that he was uncertain, even uneasy about something. Which must be a crazy thing to suppose about a man who so clearly knew his own mind. He was also a man used to having his own way. For no reason she could think of, Alex shivered.

'How about lunch?' he asked, slanting her another of his penetrating glances, as he turned the car. 'Aren't you hungry?'

She nodded, adding, before her courage failed her, 'But I don't feel like sitting on a beach.'

'Is it the sand you've taken a sudden dislike to, or me?' he enquired laconically.

'Of course not!' she protested too hastily, avoiding the eyes which rested too speculatively on her hot cheeks.

'Don't worry,' he said, 'the beach was maybe not such a good idea, after all. I don't suppose you brought a costume with you, for one thing, and a girl like you wouldn't swim without one.'

This, sounding more like criticism than praise, stung her. 'Would you want me to?' she asked sharply, as the enchanting vista of an afternoon spent lazily on a glorious Australian beach faded unhappily. With a twinge of regret she wished she hadn't dismissed his former suggestion so summarily. After being cooped up in the office and flat for over a month she could have done with some real fresh air and exercise.

She heard him replying idly, but as if he was considering her taut query seriously, 'I don't know how you like to bathe. Most girls nowadays please themselves and I don't usually argue. The decision's all yours. Of course,' he offered, straight-faced, 'I can always turn my back.'

'No, thank you,' she refused coldly, feeling incredibly like a schoolgirl and hating him for laughing at her, as he was obviously doing.

'All right,' he relented, removing his mocking eyes from her, 'perhaps some other time. A hotel will suit me nicely today.'

Alex sat very still beside him as he drove her to one. Noticing how he never hesitated or wasted time over where he was going, she wondered if he approached people in the same manner. He could be ruthless, she guessed, when he liked, and was unable to quell a growing apprehension.

The hotel he found provided them with a delicious lunch, as expensive as ever she could have wished for. Yet somehow she didn't feel as triumphant over this as she had thought she would. For her the meal dragged, each obviously high-priced mouthful threatening to choke her. Chase, on the other hand, seemed to be suffering from none of Alex's embarrassment, although he appeared to concentrate more on her than on the delectable food he was eating. He plied her with questions about her family and friends, without once repeating anything he had asked the night before. Alex wished he wouldn't, as some of them she found difficult to answer.

'Have you a special boy-friend in Sydney?' he enquired, his tone indifferent but his eyes watching her closely.

'No,' she replied, for wasn't this true, and, in this instance, she could think of no reason to lie. After this weekend she wasn't likely to be seeing Chase Marshall again.

His dark brows rose sceptically. 'You must know plenty of men, though, a pretty girl like you?'

Alex's face shadowed, giving more away to a man of Chase's brilliant intelligence than she knew. 'My mother likes entertaining and to be entertained, so we know a lot of people with sons and daughters around my age, maybe a little older. But there's no one special.' Thinking briefly of Don Fisher, she hoped her mother would forgive her for not including him in this category.

'At your age,' Chase stated dryly, 'you can afford not to be in a hurry.'

For the first time Alex felt quite grateful towards him, until she realised he was probably thinking of Ruby. Why did he think his sister should be rushed into marriage? Twenty-six was still very young. 'If you're referring to marriage,' she returned lightly, thinking it might help Ruby—if only indirectly, 'I don't intend bothering about that for a long time.'

'Or until some man changes your mind for you?' he rejoined rather tersely, as they made ready to leave.

After lunch he insisted she saw a little of the actual town. As they wandered, he pointed out parts of it and buildings which he thought might specially interest her. Then, from a stall, he brought her a beautiful bunch of long-stemmed, pale golden roses.

'Not primroses,' he presented them to her coolly, his eyes on her hair, 'but the colour matches almost exactly.'

Her cheeks flushing a delicate pink, she accepted the bouquet. His satisfaction deepened, and she suspected he took her confusion for a sign that she had already fallen for his not inconsiderable charm. Lowering her thick, curling lashes, she realised Chase was seeing the task he had set for himself almost accomplished, and the hardening of her heart also stiffened her resolve. 'Why, thank you, Mr Marshall!' Appearing to be almost overwhelmed, she hid her true thoughts behind the sweetness of a tremulous smile, and was not surprised at his approving nod, or his arrogant request that she call him Chase.

'Oh, thank you,' she smiled again, flashing him a demure glance that made her feel slightly amazed by her own endeavours and, in spite of everything, a little ashamed.

She was also amazed that he didn't suspect anything, for she was not the best of actresses and she found it virtually impossible to do as he asked and use his Christian name. In the end she improvised by calling him nothing and hoping he didn't notice. It was after six when they returned to Melbourne and she was carrying not only her flowers but a huge, expensive box of chocolates as well. Chase had also purchased a pile of the most expensive magazines and a flagon of perfume which Alex wouldn't have liked to put a price to, but when an involuntary protest had escaped her, he merely smiled and said she could share it all with Ruby. This wasn't his intention, she was sure, and was again made nervous by her own possible rashness.

It puzzled her, after this positive shower of presents, that made her feel so uncomfortably guilty, that he never once broached the question of Coolabra. He didn't even say anything about it when they reached the flat, and she wondered if he had changed his mind. Yet, glancing at all the things he had piled in her arms, she didn't think so. No man would surely spend as much on a girl if he didn't have something in view.

Before he left, as she was beginning to seriously doubt her own intelligence, he informed her autocratically, 'I rang Ruby while you were powdering your nose before lunch. We're dining with her and some of her friends tonight.'

Alex, already tense from having to prepare herself to say no to the expected renewal of his request that she should visit Coolabra, was startled into silence. She hadn't bargained for this and felt flustered. Bewildered, she stared at him, his clipped voice tightening her nerves. 'I'm not really sure I can,' she began.

The uncompromisingly straight nose and firm jawline hardened, the flare of his nostrils exhibiting barely contained anger. This, she was sure, because she hadn't immediately jumped at his invitation. It told her plainer than anything else might have done that Chase still intended to persuade her to go to his cattle station in the Outback, but that his patience was wearing thin. Her hesitation over dining with him this evening seemed to be adding fuel to the fire of his leashed frustration. Could she honestly be surprised if it leapt to a blaze? Consumed as she was by her own desire for revenge, wasn't it a fire she had done her utmost to encourage all day?

'I'm sorry,' she began again, casting around desperately in her head for the best excuse she could think of.

'You told me you had no boy-friend. Not one you considered seriously.'

Her lashes flickered, dark wands on her pale cheeks, 'It's not that . . .'

'Well, then?' Suddenly he laid a hand on her arm, his fingers grasping the softness of her skin, sending shafts of needlelike sensation shooting almost painfully through her slender body. It startled her, making her tremble.

Deliberately Chase leant nearer, as though very sure she couldn't continue resisting him. His eyes held hers, his own warmer as he subdued his temper. 'You've enjoyed yourself today, haven't you, Alex?'

'Yes.' Her lips were stiff, but she made no attempt to deny it. Underneath all her tension and uncertainty she had enjoyed herself in a way.

'Then,' he said, letting go of her while his eyes narrowed thoughtfully, 'I'll see you later, about eight.'

CHAPTER THREE

As he got in his car, Chase lifted his hand in a brief gesture of farewell. 'You'll be coming to the hotel with Ruby, but I'll see you home myself.'

Later when they met he was warm and friendly, as though they had never shared even a moment's dissent. His was an effortless charm, Alex realised, conscious of its effect on the other women in the party as well as on herself. She felt grateful for having been forewarned of his true opinion of her. Otherwise, if she hadn't known of it, she might have succumbed as eagerly as the others apparently did.

It was this knowledge which, as before, drove her to revengeful lengths she would never normally have contemplated. When Chase asked her to dance, after dinner, she let her slight body curve closely to his. She even made herself smile at him, slowly and rather seductively, in a way she had seen others doing but had never yet tried on a man herself. As though conducting a slightly breathless experiment, she watched for results and was satisfied, if a little apprehensive, to find his eyes darkening and his arms tightening. But when warning bells rang clearly in her head, she dismissed them derisively. If she couldn't handle a man at her age, she never would!

Chase had promised to take her home himself and he did. Ruby didn't accompany them but went on to a friend's house for coffee. Alexander hadn't been with her tonight, and Alex wondered if this was the beginning of Chase's campaign. It might be far-fetched, but she had the distinct impression that he had made very sure that everyone at the dinner party had known she was called Alex, and that she shared the flat with Ruby. Again suspecting she was being used, Alex felt an odd mixture of misery and anger. Ruby, however, hadn't seemed in the least put out. In fact she had been quite remarkably gay all evening.

When Chase stopped the car outside the flat and turned to her, Alex expected him to ask about Coolabra again, but he didn't. Under different circumstances she might have put him out of his misery once and for all, but, still smarting from his insults, she was determined to say nothing until he did. If he had to continue wasting his precious time, it would only make him more furious in the end. And this was Alex's main objective, at the moment, that the great Chase Marshall should learn a lesson he wouldn't easily forget. As it was, the effort of being pleasant to someone who bored him must be costing him plenty. He wasn't a man to appreciate what was quite clearly a slightly ridiculous situation.

When he asked if she was doing anything particular next day, she was surprised into shaking her head.

'Then why not spend it with me, Alex?' he smiled, taking hold of her hand and raising it to his mouth.

At his touch, her assumed sophistication deserted her and she almost jumped. His arms around her, earlier, as they danced after dinner, had been more than enough. His mouth on her palm, the warm, sensual strength of it, was too much. With a half strangled cry, as fire ran rampant through her, she jerked her hand away.

Then, with alarm, as she suddenly remembered what she must do, she tried to smile. It wasn't the kind of smile she sought, it was a wobbly, tentative smile, which held more than a hint of confusion, yet strangely enough it seemed to please Chase. His hard face cleared, a trace of dissatisfaction leaving it, as he lifted his head to find her eyes dilating nervously. This time he repeated his question more gently.

'If you like,' she whispered, the best she could do with her breath still hard to find.

'Good,' he said briefly.

He arranged a time to pick her up, and they spent the whole of the next day together. He knew of a good beach, miles away from anywhere along the coast, which proved every bit as good as he said. They had it to themselves.

'It's maybe not as perfect as some of the islands on the Great Barrier Reef,' he smiled, 'but it should be quite adequate for a few hours.'

'I haven't ever been to the Barrier Reef,' she admitted ruefully.

'I could take you if you like,' he teased softly, his eyes on her shapely young figure. She was wearing a yellow bikini, consisting of two scraps of material, which she hadn't felt selfconscious in before. Now, funnily enough, when Chase Marshall looked her over with unstinted admiration in his eyes, she did. His close regard made her pulses behave uncomfortably.

'Really, Mr Marshall,' she retorted, keeping a wary grip on her senses, 'you make one rule for your sister and another for other girls!'

'I wasn't suggesting anything improper,' he laughed. 'You're too quick off the mark, Miss Latham. I merely had in mind a trip from Coolabra. It's not very far.'

'Always supposing I get to Coolabra,' she retorted, attempting to set him down quietly.

'Oh, come, Alex,' he sighed, quite clearly disinclined to take her seriously, 'we're playing a little game, you and I, and to a certain extent, it's been very enjoyable. But you know, and I know, you'll be there.'

So it had come—the final showdown. Regret touched her sadly. She had been so delighted with the beach, its glorious isolation, that she would have given anything to have avoided a confrontation right now. But it was here, and there was no way she could sidestep such a leading statement.

Yet even now she tried to, by being indefinite. 'I'm sorry,' she faltered, wishing she sounded more emphatic.

'You'll be sorrier still if you miss such a trip,' he warned, his eyes holding hers narrowly. 'Don't make any mistake about it, Alex, Coolabra is quite something.'

Finding his unmistakable blaze of pride formidable, she placed a protective hand over the betraying pulse in her throat. 'I can't argue about that, of course, but I'm not your sister, you know. You can't order me around as you like, or blackmail me into obeying you.'

'There are other ways.' Supremely confident, he moved nearer, his brief black trunks exposing whipcord muscles and fuzz-covered chest. He had a light covering of hair on his limbs too, she noticed, as her glance travelled, driven by a panicky fascination, right down the length of him to his long powerful legs. His superb physique made her heart beat faster, and it was humiliating to realise he could see the rapid rise and fall of it in her breast. His eyes stayed on it, scrutinising mockingly, without apparent shame, while Alex, suddenly incapable of movement, couldn't turn away.

Yet he made no attempt to actually touch her. Alex, who had never given herself to a man yet, or wanted to, knew instinctively that this wasn't what Chase was asking. He was simply threatening mildly. He was well aware that threats were often all that was necessary in order to get one's own way, especially when applied to someone as innocent as the girl beside him. But Alex was afraid that if he should try to go further she wouldn't be able to resist him.

As he studied the slender yet sensuously curved lines of her body he seemed also to be reading her mind. His eyes were glinting, summing up her fluctuating colour. He saw how her pupils expanded with heightening emotion, making the starry blue of the iris seem to spill over to tint the white. How her full, tenderly shaped mouth was beginning to tremble and soften, without her being conscious of it.

'Alex,' his breath rasped slightly, 'I don't think you've ever had a shattering love affair. I don't believe you've had much experience of anything. You're such a Sleeping Beauty that I can't fight you, or tempt you in the usual way. Not yet.'

Angrily she broke in, his curt observations jerking her from the lethargy which was beginning to attack her. 'You can't be saying that if I was the right sort of woman—another sort of woman,' she corrected, 'you'd be prepared to sleep with me to get me to agree to going to Coolabra?'

'Oh, God!' incensed, he leant over to grasp her shrinking shoulders, his fingers digging unremorsefully into her flesh. 'I could smack you for that! I was simply hinting that another woman might have found me attractive enough to think it worthwhile spending a few weeks up there, with no strings attached. She'd be well paid into the bargain, I'd see to that.'

For what, exactly? Alex wondered, her mind already too confused. It wasn't as if Chase was going to be around. He might talk as though he would be, but hadn't he told Ruby he would only be staying two days? Any payment he offered would be the same as she was already getting in the office, as, technically, she would still be working. With supreme egotism he must be offering himself as a bribe. Once she was nicely settled in at Coolabra he would simply disappear. For a man of his deviousness it would be easy. He probably wouldn't even bother to make an excuse!

Fortunately she was old enough not to fall for such tactics. Glancing at him stubbornly, she fell back on her trump card, the one which made all Chase's arguments irrelevant. 'You forget I'm not due for a holiday, so even if I wanted to go I couldn't.'

'It could be arranged. This is a good season to go visiting up north. The weather's getting cooler all the time.'

'So it might be,' she allowed her eyes to widen wistfully, 'but you wouldn't expect me to walk out on my job. I might get another, but I like this one very much.'

'After a few weeks?' His mouth took on a cynical quirk as he looked at her. 'I can arrange for you to be away.'

'You?'

'Yes. I would rather you'd gone voluntarily to the head of your department yourself and been willing to receive the leave he would have graciously granted. Then you need never have known that the office more or less belongs to me.'

'I'm impressed.' She was actually shaken. To hide it she stared stubbornly out to sea. The foam-tipped waves were breaking on the white virgin sands. As her heart might be breaking, if she didn't watch out. 'Do you always manage to arrange other people's lives so easily?' she asked.

'Sometimes I know what's good for them, better than they do themselves.'

'Like Ruby?' Bringing her eyes back to him she tried to match his crispness, not altogether succeeding.

He nodded. 'And you.'

Alex drew a small furious breath. Was he daring to assume he could read her like a book? 'I'm sorry, Mr Marshall, but no matter what you're prepared to do I still won't agree. Besides, Ruby and I aren't very close.'

'She has helped you, though?'

She could see he was annoyed and wondered why she could both anger and bore him. It stood out a mile that she did, easily demonstrated by his hard-held impatience. Come to think of it—Alex scuffled a perplexed toe in the sand—she wasn't sure why she was being so intense over it all. In her own way, mightn't she be just as unreasonable as he was? Yet pride, such as she had never known before, held her in an inexorable grip and she couldn't fight it. 'How many times do I have to tell you I won't change my mind?' she said primly. 'Of course I'm grateful for all you intended doing for me,' she finished, sweetly ironical, 'and for Ruby's help.'

Suddenly Chase shrugged, his hands, which had left her quivering shoulders, lifting in a gesture of surprising indifference. 'Let's forget about it, then. I refuse to waste an entire weekend arguing with a beautiful girl. You may decide to come to Coolabra yet.'

Beneath his cool gaze Alex felt very young and didn't know where she found the strength to continue defying him. If it hadn't been for the remarks she had overheard, would she have been able to? Now, one more remark he had added to the list helped strengthen her resolve not to be swayed by his undoubted attractiveness. He had declared decisively that a word from him would be enough to release her from the office. Wasn't it time someone said no to him and meant it?

All the time they swam she kept her distance, even while she was aware of an increasing desire to be near him. When he did come close, his powerful limbs cutting effortlessly through the water, her heart would begin reacting uncomfortably and she would move away, hating the open mockery in his eyes as she did so.

Later, they dined out again. Alex was surprised, after their conversation earlier on the beach, that Chase bothered to ask her. She was even more confused when he asserted that there was no need to go back home and change. They would dine as they were.

Doubtfully, she agreed, telling herself firmly that it didn't matter how she looked, but knowing all the time it did, at least to her. Chase might tell her that her fair hair and sand-hazed skin had a bloom that was wonderful, but she wasn't so sure. She thought his eyes stayed on her almost continually because she looked more like a sea-washed oddity than anything else!

Always, no matter what he wore, Chase managed to look superior. His good looks were outstanding. His face was hard, as was his decisive jaw, while his dark eyes never missed a thing. Alex was glad he was leaving Melbourne immediately, as she might not be able to hold out against him indefinitely, for all her pride shrieked loudly that she had more reason to now than ever.

Pride stiffened her resolve again as they reached the flat and he unexpectedly bent over her. 'This has to be goodbye,' he said softly, 'but it's been nice knowing you. In fact, I'm beginning to realise I might be going to miss you. Don't you think you're going to miss me, Alex?'

'No!' she gasped, outraged by his audacity as he swiftly bent his dark head. His breath was on her mouth before his mouth swerved to descend on her cheek. It was a chaste kiss, one which he might have bestowed on the aunt whom Ruby said looked after them, but she knew he meant it deviously, as a reminder of what she would be missing.

As he feathered her face lightly, but as though his lips were surprisingly reluctant to leave it, she felt his strong body tense. For a moment it was as if he had been struck by lightning, for she had the hazy impression, as a sudden heat leapt from his mouth to fuse them together, that he was tensely fighting an urge stronger than anything he had ever known. That at some point the lesson he had set out to teach had rebounded, in some far from welcome way, upon himself.

Alex felt an urge within herself too. A driving, confusing desire to turn in his arms, to have them closely around her, to curve her own about his neck, to feel the full force of his dominating mouth against her own. It was only when her breasts went taut, an achingly unfamiliar sensation, that alarm whipped through her, causing her to draw back breathlessly. She was much too grateful that something had saved her from making a complete fool of herself to understand what had been happening to her.

Their eyes met, clinging for long enigmatical seconds while Alex found her voice. 'Goodnight and goodbye, Chase,' she whispered, a strangled sound which she wished could have been an angry shout, as she almost thrust herself from his car. It didn't help that his own brief farewell was mockingly harsh as she slammed the door.

In her bedroom, Alex sank down on her bed, her head whirling. She felt slightly sick, every pulse in her body seemed to be throbbing. All this she tried to dismiss as the result of fright, but there was no comfort to be gained from knowing Chase Marshall could affect her so strongly. She had been kissed before, but never had she felt like this.

It couldn't be that she was attracted to him. Why should she feel attracted towards a man who roamed from one place to another, treating women so casually? He probably ate little girls like herself for breakfast! No woman with any looks at all might be safe from him. It was crazy to wish she could have known him better. More intimately, an inner voice taunted, yet so persistently that she jumped up with relief when the telephone rang.

Because Chase hadn't had time to get back to his apartment, she knew it couldn't be him. Thinking of this, she managed to pick up the receiver with a relatively steady hand. Dully she gave the flat number.

'Alex darling, is that you?'

It was her mother. A few minutes later Alex replaced the receiver, this time with her hand shaking. She was altogether stunned, both by herself and the news she had received.

Her mother had said she was coming to Melbourne at the end of the week with her English friend, and Don Fisher would be bringing them. He would also be staying with them. Tomorrow he was booking their accommodation. His father was giving him a few days off, specially. And—Mrs Latham's voice had dropped to the level of that used when secrets are being triumphantly betrayed—Don was bringing a ring, one of the most beautiful she had ever seen.

'His father's a really big name in Sydney now, Alex,' she had continued complacently. 'You could scarcely do better, and he told me personally that he approves of you and Don being married. He would like Don to settle down and have a family.'

'But I can't marry Don Fisher!' Alex had gasped. 'For one thing, I don't love him.'

Her mother said, 'Nonsense, darling!' in the exact tones she used when squashing opposition on one of her committees. 'Don will soon help you change your mind.'

'I won't be here.'

'Not there?' Mrs Latham's voice had grown colder. 'Why not, pray?'

'I——' with great difficulty Alex steadied her own voice, which was rising like an octave out of control, 'I have to go north for the—the firm.'

'North?'

'Yes,' Alex improvised wildly. 'They need extra help in the office, on one of the larger cattle stations. It sometimes happens, you know, and I can't refuse.'

Heaven forgive me, she prayed silently, in the sudden silence. Or help me, she readjusted her prayer as she realised this meant she had burnt her boats, so to speak, and would have to go to Coolabra, after all. If Chase Marshall hadn't changed his mind about taking her. She might have to beg. She almost groaned aloud at the prospect, but wouldn't anything be better than staying in Melbourne and becoming engaged to Don Fisher? That she didn't love him might count for nothing against the combined weight of his and her mother's persuasions.

'Do you know how long you'll be away?' Mrs Latham sounded both suspicious and cross.

'Maybe two or three weeks, I'm not sure.' Alex drew a deep breath. 'If you like you can ring the office here in Melbourne.'

'Oh, well,' grudgingly, 'I suppose if it's only for a short time, but Don's going to be very disappointed. I'll get him to ring your office later in the month to ask when you'll be back. I think you should seriously consider handing in your notice and coming home.'

'I'll think about it,' Alex heard herself murmuring in a cowardly way, as usual shrinking from all-out opposition. Anything could happen, must happen, in the next few weeks. If she liked the north she might even look for a job in Darwin. Anything to escape her mother's clutches without a lot of unpleasantness.

It was far from easy to ring Chase and tell him she had changed her mind. Ruby had his number scribbled down on a pad and Alex sat staring at it for a long time before finding sufficient courage to contact him. He would naturally believe those few moments she had spent in his arms had made her think again. He had only kissed her cheek, yet his experience was such that he must have gauged the depth of her response. She could only hope it wasn't something he would ever be tempted to try again. Wishing her heart would stop beating so unevenly, she began dialling.

'Yes?' he answered, so curtly, she almost shrank.

'Alex Latham, Mr Marshall. I—I've decided I'd like to come to Coolabra after all.'

A short silence suggested that he was startled, but of course he never would be—about anything. 'This is a sudden change,' he remarked dryly. 'Why?'

She didn't want to go into that. It would involve Don Fisher and her mother. How could she explain to someone like Chase Marshall what her mother was like? Or about Don? Chase would simply laugh. And while she didn't mind about Don, for her father's sake if nothing else, she couldn't bear having Chase laughing about her mother. It was the same old sense of loyalty, she supposed, rearing its familiar head, but she was never able to ignore it.

Despairingly she tried to gloss over it. 'I did change my mind suddenly, I'll admit. I'm a bit like that . . .'

'It's always interesting to know,' he returned sardonically, while giving no indication as to what he thought of her change of mind, in this instance.

Hastily she said, 'My mother has just called and I told her I was going to Coolabra.'

'You're taking a lot for granted, aren't you? After the way you refused me only a few minutes ago?'

'Then you don't want me . . .?'

'I didn't say that.' He paused decisively. 'You're necessary, to straighten things out for Ruby.'

Alex swallowed at his frankness, but caution warned her to make the best of it. 'You said you'd be able to fix things at the office?'

'Yes. You can leave everything to me, now that I know for sure. Thank you, Miss Latham. I'll be in touch.'

Fancying he sounded slightly contemptuous, she slowly replaced the receiver. It was obvious that he was convinced she had intended going with Ruby from the beginning and had only pretended otherwise so as to get what she could out of him. She wished she could have brought herself to tell him she was only going to Coolabra in order to escape being pushed into an engagement she didn't want. That she had let him spend money on her this weekend only because she had overheard him saying she bored him. Now, as often happened when looking back, she wished she had ignored what he had said. If she hadn't gone out with him he would never have held her as he had done in the car, and she was sure that if this should complicate her stay at Coolabra in any way, she would only have herself to blame!

Three rather turbulent days later she was at Coolabra. Ruby and she flew up to Alice Springs where they were met by the station manager and taken to Coolabra in Chase Marshall's private plane.

'One of them,' Ruby informed her, glancing with surprise at Alex's wide-eyed face. 'He travels everywhere by plane and has several.'

Alex, like the average Australian, was no stranger to air travel, but she hadn't ever flown in a small plane. As they left Alice Springs, the famous town in the Centre, she felt decidedly apprehensive.

Ruby said unkindly. 'You'd better relax, otherwise you might never make it.'

Drew Blake, the station manager, smiled at her kindly, keenly aware of the nervousness which darkened eyes more vividly blue than any he had ever seen before. The frank admiration in his own might have been enough to give confidence to the average girl, but he added a few words to it. 'We tend to wobble about a bit on the air currents, but believe me, you could be running more risk on the track down there.'

Alex, glancing beneath them, saw the Stuart Highway winding its endless way north to Darwin and ruefully closed her eyes. Opening them again immediately, she smiled at the lean, suntanned man at the controls who kept glancing at her anxiously. 'I hope I'll make it!'

'It just takes time,' he drawled. 'It just takes time.'

She believed him, but didn't point out that she wouldn't have much time. Only two or three weeks at the most, according to Ruby, who still grumbled about having to come at all. For all this, under her bored veneer of sophistication, Alex felt Ruby was rather pleased about something. Once she had caught the other girl's eyes positively dancing, when she thought no one was looking.

Drew Blake was a youngish man in his thirties, with a pleasantly good-looking face. Ruby began talking to him. 'I don't know why Chase is going to so much trouble, Drew, dragging me back home. Alex and I were going to the Reef.' She didn't seem at all bothered that this was the first time Alex had ever heard her mention it.

'We don't question your brother, Ruby,' Drew replied. 'I dare say he has his reasons.'

'Is he still at Coolabra?'

Drew laughed. 'He only arrived yesterday. I'll just say this, he talks about staying.'

'Usually he only stays a couple of days—you must have misunderstood.'

Alex listened with mixed feelings, her interest torn between Chase Marshall and the view below her. She got the impression of a barren landscape, a desolate, barren land, but one possessed of a strange and haunting beauty. Occasionally a few trees or a lonely homestead stood out like sentinels on the bare red earth which was covered by saltbush and spinifex. The distances were immense, a wilderness of plains and remote ranges, dry river valleys and stony terrain, and over it all hung a vapour of afternoon heat that hazed the limitless horizon.

How far was that horizon? Alex, straining her eyes towards it, couldn't make out, but she would have liked to have known. Chase would have told her, she felt sure. On their trips out from Melbourne he had been a mine of information. Apart from an hour, when he had arrived at his sister's flat with air tickets and instructions, she hadn't seen him for three days. It surely wasn't possible that she was missing him?

Beneath them a herd of Santa Gertrudis cattle sud-

denly seemed to appear, men on horseback with them.
Drew told her, 'That's Dintlaw Downs. I wonder how
many of ours they've got?'

Ruby smiled idly without replying, as though Drew's
remark was too familiar to need comment. It seemed to
tell Alex two things—that someone was stealing Chase
Marshall's cattle and that they must be getting near
Coolabra. Two things she found slightly alarming.

'Don't you ever do anything about it? If the cattle are
being stolen, I mean,' she asked Drew, her voice slightly
incredulous.

'Oh,' he grinned, poker-faced, 'I wouldn't go so far as
to say those fellows down there are criminals! We have
our little arrangements, that usually work all right, to
the satisfaction of everyone concerned. It's not like it
used to be.'

'Not always,' retorted Ruby dryly.

Feeling frustrated because of things she didn't understand, but which the other two clearly thought too com-
monplace to need explaining, Alex was glad to hear
Drew's whoop of satisfaction.

'There she is, Miss Ruby. Coolabra!'

While Ruby remarked coldly that she hadn't been
away for years, Alex drew her breath in sharply on catching her first glimpse of Coolabra from the air. From
here it looked like a field of English mushrooms, that
she could still remember, spread out in white clumps.
Nearer she saw a large homestead surrounded by trees
with other buildings and yards scattered around it at
varying distances. Even at her first sight of it something
clutched at her heart, threatening never to let go. It was
as if a place down there had been waiting all her life for
her, ready to welcome her with open arms.

Ruby's sharply voiced opinion of Alex's rapt expression was no more scornful than Alex's own silent one.
She had always considered herself to be sane and well
balanced and made an effort to pull herself together.

Swiftly she lowered her lashes to hide her telltale eyes and took another deep breath.

The plane circled, landing some distance from the homestead, very stylishly, as though Drew felt he was bringing in royalty and wished to make an impression. They bumped slightly on the plane's first contact with the ground, but she could tell it was an expert landing. When they came to a standstill, Ruby was on her feet within seconds, well used to small planes and suffering no ill effects. Alex didn't think she did, but her legs felt slightly unsteady as she groped her way out after Ruby and Drew.

Blinking in the strong sunlight, she saw a utility approaching at speed, Chase Marshall at the wheel. Bemused, her gaze remained fixed on him. She had known he was here but hadn't expected him to be on the runway meeting them. As he stopped and slid from behind the wheel, she noticed he was wearing a pair of moleskin trousers, with a checked shirt and wide-brimmed hat. At once he looked different—more authoritative, if this were possible, than he had done in Melbourne. The clothes he wore, fitting closely to his tall body, seemed to lend strength to the sheer impact of his vital personality, which she had already been too aware of in the city.

She was conscious of Drew turning to assist her, his smile warmly concerned on her suddenly tense face. Then he was curtly brushed aside and Chase was helping her to the ground.

'Good afternoon, Alex. Welcome to Coolabra.' His glance went slowly over her delicate fairness. Closely he studied the faint shadows of stress under her eyes, the slight beading of perspiration on the wide, intelligent brow and provocative upper lip. Narrowly he came back to her eyes, and for a short space of time Alex felt they had the world to themselves.

Ruby broke in impatiently, not used to being ignored, even by her brother. 'Alex is quite capable of looking after herself, Chase. She may look breakable, but believe me, she isn't.'

Turning on her curtly, Chase snapped, 'Any fool could see she was ready to fall from the plane. This kind of flying takes getting used to.'

'I suppose so.' Indifferently Ruby walked towards the truck, leaving Alex to follow, while Chase and Drew started on the luggage.

Alex hadn't brought a lot, but she thought what she had packed would be suitable. It was a whole lot warmer here than in Melbourne, and while she could feel herself responding to the heat she longed to get into something cooler.

Ruby said she had better ride in the back of the truck, which she did. Whether this arrangement pleased Chase or not, he didn't say. Alex couldn't tell, as he got in the driving seat and swung round to look at her, for his eyes were cool and expressionless. Only his mouth seemed to suggest a momentary anger as it hardened to a straight line as, for no reason she could think of, he stared intently at her.

When they reached the house she met Miss Marshall, the aunt who looked after it for Chase. She was a true autocrat, in her late sixties and still very good-looking. Her kindly face was full of character and Alex suspected she would be a good judge of it.

Like Chase, she noticed the slight strain on Alex's sensitive young face and took charge immediately.

'Ruby, you'd better take Miss Latham upstairs right away. I've put her in the pink guest room.' Though slightly puzzled by Ruby's disdainfully raised eyebrows, she added, 'I'll get Mrs Young to serve tea in half an hour, which should give you both plenty of time to freshen up.'

Chase, after making Alex known to his aunt, had disappeared, but when Alex came down again he was sitting with Miss Marshall in the drawing-room, to which Alex had been directed by a smiling Aboriginal girl.

'Come in, my dear,' Harriet Marshall waved her hand. 'Where's Ruby?'

'She doesn't want tea . . .' Alex sat rather nervously on the chair Miss Marshall indicated, very conscious of Chase.

'Doesn't want to give an account of herself, more likely,' Miss Marshall retorted tartly. 'Have you told her, Chase,' she turned to her nephew, 'that Henry's coming over later?'

'Not yet,' he replied laconically, his eyes on Alex. She had changed into a strapped sundress, just bare enough to be cool without being too daring.

His mouth quirked. Was he laughing at her modesty? Raising challenging eyes to him, she flushed and felt foolish on meeting only a cool surveillance. Of course, he wouldn't feel anything, one way or another, for a girl who bored him!

CHAPTER FOUR

CHASE's next words took Alex by surprise. 'What do you think of my home, Alex?'

Glancing at him quickly, she received the rather unbelievable impression that her answer was of some importance to him. His dark gaze was intent, probing hers, as though he looked for inner reactions that he might weigh against the usual conventional reply he expected from her.

Because of this, she answered guardedly, 'I haven't really had time yet.' Then, unable to help herself, she exclaimed impulsively, her blue eyes shining, 'I think it's wonderful! I've never seen anything like it before.'

'You mean the house?'

Her glance fell to the cup she was holding, hiding her quick dismay. Naturally he would believe she had seen only the house. That this was indescribable she couldn't deny. It had comfort and style, vastly superior to anything she had ever known. Even so, she had sense enough to realise it was enough to impress and delight even a woman used only to the best. Chase would be convinced a girl like herself would never notice anything else.

She nodded to his query with a tentative smile. 'The house is beautiful, of course, but I didn't know about it when I first saw Coolabra.'

'You mean you were impressed from the air?' he sounded coolly amused.

'If you like.' Her eyes widened on him with a faint dislike. 'You don't have to laugh! I don't suppose I'm your first visitor to be hit by something inexplicable

59

when looking down from up there, but I'm sure every earthly paradise has its snags.'

Softly he drawled, 'Don't look at me as though I'm the biggest one, Alex. If you say you fell in love with Coolabra at first sight, I'd be the last to disapprove, but don't get carried away by first impressions. Coolabra is too big to see all at once. There's more to it than meets the eye.'

'Yes,' Miss Marshall smiled, with some pride, 'over five thousand square miles of it, and this is only one of our stations.'

'Ruby mentioned that Coolabra is part of a company,' said Alex.

'Chase is the company, dear,' his aunt rejoined mildly, but with obvious admiration. 'He runs everything.' When neither of her two listeners replied, she smiled at Alex again. 'How long have you known Ruby, Miss Latham?'

'Alex works in the same office,' Chase explained before Alex could draw breath. 'They share the flat—or have done since Miss Beck left.'

'Ah, yes,' Miss Marshall was immediately diverted, 'that was an extraordinary affair, wasn't it? Imagine anyone being so swept off their feet!' she appealed to Alex when Chase made no comment. 'Don't you think it was extraordinary, dear, to fall for a man just like that?'

'As Alex hasn't been in love yet, it's no use asking her.' Softly derisive, Chase stared at Alex, clearly waiting for her delicate flush.

He wasn't disappointed and Alex hated his easy ability to disturb her. Indignantly she protested as she met his eyes, 'It doesn't stop me from using my imagination.'

'Oh, I think you've plenty of that,' he countered mockingly, holding her eyes with his. 'But perhaps, like Miss Beck, you should be putting your dreams into practice. She must have discovered that life is really made for living. And one doesn't have to be in love.'

Alex was thankful when tea was over, as she seemed to arouse Chase Marshall's disparagement at every turn. When he was called away she fancied even his aunt gave a small sigh of relief.

'Chase has too much to do,' the older woman said, as if seeking to excuse his abruptness. 'I'm always hoping that one day he'll meet some nice girl and settle down. I'm sure if he had a wife and family to keep him here, he'd be willing to delegate some of his work, in other parts of the country.'

'Doesn't he have a special girl-friend?' Ruby had hinted that there was one and Alex couldn't understand why her curiosity was driving her to ask again. It hadn't anything to do with her and she suspected Chase wouldn't be pleased if he were to discover his aunt had been discussing him like this.

'He had someone until recently,' Miss Marshall replied tartly. 'A film star, of all things. Not the kind of girl who would ever settle down here.'

While Alex's heart dropped, she forced herself to go on, 'You never know. She might.'

'Well, whether she would or not doesn't arise, my dear. Chase has told me himself it's all over and has promised he'll try to find a more sensible girl.'

'Sensible girls are often considered dull,' Alex said dryly, somehow not able to see Chase with this kind of girl at all.

She was startled, though, when Miss Marshall retorted, 'Exactly what he said, and he made it sound like a warning. However, nothing could be worse than Davina. Only I hope he hasn't left it too late.'

'Too late?' Chase was one of the most attractive men Alex had ever seen, and in the prime of life at thirty-six.

Miss Marshall shrugged. 'I'm not really talking about age, dear. Women find him very attractive, but he seldom seems to take them seriously. Often I find myself wondering now if he ever will.'

Later, during dinner, Alex felt her eyes wandering frequently in Chase's direction. She didn't know why she should find him so riveting as she was still sore from the frank remarks he had passed earlier. She wished she could forget them, but somehow she could not. These, added to those he had already made about her being malleable and boring, hurt. But perhaps it was just as well she knew his exact opinion of her. At least it would keep her from missing him when he left. A few unkind words might make an admirable barricade to hide behind when other, more heartshaking thoughts bombarded her too vulnerable senses.

Chase sat at one end of the long gleaming dining table, his aunt at the other. Both wore an air of supreme confidence. Alex couldn't imagine anyone defying either of them and getting away with it. Miss Marshall talked a lot, a woman who clearly enjoyed having people around her. Her dress was smart and must have cost quite as much as Ruby's, her hair was exquisitely styled, but otherwise she made no attempt to disguise her age. Alex suspected she was in many ways an old-fashioned woman, in so much that she would have high principles.

Chase, as host, was charming; a little aloof yet missing nothing. When his eyes rested on her, Alex was glad she had managed to find time to buy a new dress herself before leaving Melbourne, and that the creamy georgette she wore this evening was more flattering than anything she had ever possessed. It moulded to her figure, and while the neckline was low it was still circumspect. She did wish, though, that Chase's eyes wouldn't return so frequently to the shadowed hollow between her half exposed breasts. It made her feel peculiar, in a way she wasn't sure she liked. She had a feeling that he deliberately meant to disturb her and didn't really mind how he went about it.

Henry Brett, who was sitting beside Ruby, had ar-

rived in time for dinner. After attending a meeting in
Brisbane he had been held up. When he first arrived, he
had certainly given every appearance of being angry,
but after he had talked with Ruby and met Alex his
mood appeared to brighten. Alex felt cynically amused
as Ruby repeated her name more often than was necessary, and Henry's face lightened with relief. For all this,
Alex felt Ruby might have a lot more explaining to do
later and couldn't feel altogether sorry for her. Mr Brett
looked like a man who had recently come—or been
brought—to his senses, and Alex couldn't help wondering what, or who, had been indirectly responsible.

After dinner, when Henry asked if he could borrow a
utility to take Ruby for a ride in the moonlight, Chase
agreed genially. Half an hour afterwards Chase excused
himself too, to go to the office, and Mrs Marshall went
to speak to the housekeeper. Left on her own and feeling curiously lonely, Alex decided to have a short walk
in the garden before going to bed. She didn't think she
would sleep unless she got some fresh air.

As she stepped from the house to the garden the
night air, after the heat of the day, seemed wonderfully
cool and fresh. Gratefully she took long deep breaths of
it. She could see nothing of the moon Henry had mentioned, but the stars were huge above her head, much
brighter, she was sure, than those in the south. With a
sigh of contentment she choose a wide path which
meandered around small groups of what seemed in the
darkness to be shrubs. As she hadn't yet explored the
garden or anywhere else, she thought she would be
wiser not to go very far and risk getting lost.

She hadn't been out more than ten minutes and was
thinking of going back before she could be missed,
when Chase came up behind her. Not really pleased to
see him, she said quickly, 'I was just going in.'

'Surely not?' lazily he smiled at her. 'You've only
been out a few minutes. I nearly suggested we went with
Ruby and Henry, but we might have been de trop.'

Looking up at him, Alex tried to see the harsh features above hers more clearly. 'You're awfully casual about it. Do you think he's really going to forgive her?'

Again he smiled. 'Henry has apparently decided there's nothing much to forgive, but a little indiscretion, which you've put right simply by being here.'

Incensed, Alex retorted fiercely, 'And you don't mind being part of this deception? What's it going to be called? The fooling of Henry?'

'You're awfully prickly of a sudden,' he drawled. 'Why the temper? Ruby might have intended to, but she never actually got around to doing anything. As far as I can see you haven't had to tell any lies. You told him you worked in the same office as Ruby and that seemed to satisfy him. I doubt if he'll ask you outright about the holiday you were supposed to be having together. He won't want to remind Ruby of it. Unless I'm mistaken he'll be concentrating on a honeymoon.'

'So—if they come back engaged, I can go home?'

'No, not yet. You're being too hasty.' Chase paused sardonically. 'He's not that daft. You have to be here to convince other people, but don't worry. It will all be done so deviously you won't be aware of anything happening. Henry's parents might want to meet you and there'll be a party or two, that's all.'

'Then they'll be married?'

'I'll eat my hat, Alex, if they don't. It seems we've brought them both back to their senses, if by different routes.'

'Do you always get your own way?' she asked sharply.

'If possible,' he said with unpardonable conceit. 'I'd like to know why you changed your mind about coming here. I'd like to think it came under the heading of getting my own way, too. It bothers me that I'm not so sure.'

Uneasily, she glanced away from him. 'You're quite right. It had nothing to do with you personally—but I can't explain.'

'You might have to one day.'

Diplomatically Alex let that pass. It was unlikely they would share anything in the future.

His eyes were on her averted face. 'I'm curious, but I won't press you. You're clearly not ready to share your secrets with me yet.'

Lightly she said, 'Other people's secrets can be disappointing.'

'I agree, but I might enjoy yours.' His glance concentrated through the darkness, as the light wind lifted the soft golden hair, exposing her perfect profile, the beautiful lines of her head and throat. His voice roughened slightly, he said, 'I would like to know all about you, both mentally and physically.'

She wasn't quite sure what he meant, but something inside her stirred uneasily, like an early warning system against invasion. 'Wouldn't you be afraid I might bore you?' she asked innocently.

Chase laughed, so she couldn't be sure that he considered her question seriously. 'If I let you keep your secrets, and you allow me to keep mine, that needn't stop us from getting to know each other better.'

'What's the point, though?' A ferment of uncertainty inside her, she looked up at him. 'You're only staying two days and I'll soon be gone myself. I suppose we're like ships which pass in the night.'

'Even if we were to know each other only two hours, Alex, I would rather it was on a friendly footing. And plans can be changed. I come and go as I please.'

Alex's voice was unsteady as she challenged him. 'You always leave a way out? You believe in playing safe.'

His mocking smile held the hint of a threat. 'No, indeed I do not, but I suspect you do.'

As she felt her cheeks grow warm, Alex was glad that the darkness must hide her quick flush. 'Isn't it wiser for a girl to play safe? Emotions can be messy things, from what I've seen.'

Firmly he replied, 'They can also provide us with a great deal of pleasure, if handled properly.'

Greatly daring, she retorted. 'Being a man, I imagine, you always relate emotions with sex?'

'Why not?' Although his brows rose, his eyes held a glimmer of amusement. 'That can be very enjoyable as well, as I think you have yet to find out?'

'I suppose so,' she replied frankly. 'I think it's better not to experiment before marriage. In spite of what you say I still believe that the problems might outweigh the pleasure.'

Ironically he smiled. 'I wasn't advocating letting it all run riot, but keeping everything on too tight a rein can make for a very dull life—and people.'

'Would you say I was dull?'

'No.' He disregarded her slightly anxious indignation. 'You've a lot to learn, Alex Latham, but you've a lot to give. You can deny it until sun-up, but it's there in your eyes and mouth—the perfect shape of you. A mouth gives a lot away, you know, and yours, I would be willing to bet, would be capable of giving more away than you bargained for.'

'Don't be ridiculous!' She stepped back sharply, angry rather than frightened. 'I don't even recognise the girl you're describing.'

'Don't you?' he asked silkily.

She moved quickly and stumbled, feeling she must get away from him. Automatically his hand shot out to steady her, and the warmth of her skin combined with the coldness of her voice must have woken a devil in him. Swiftly he caught her close to his hard, masculine body.

While her heart raced he said softly, 'I think it's high time you learnt a few things about yourself. If they aren't helped, sleeping beauties are apt to fall over their own feet.'

'I don't want any lessons from you!' she gasped.

Gently threatening, he brushed back some fine strands of golden hair which the wind had blown across her mouth. 'In situations like this I'm apt to concentrate on what I want, but I'd be surprised if we didn't both want the same thing.'

His hand had made feathery movements against her lips. Now he lowered his dark head to touch his mouth to where his fingers had been.

Caught off balance, she gasped and would have jerked back if his arm had given even a fraction. As she tried to escape his arms tightened, his mouth hardening, as if her resistance angered him, making him regret his gentle approach. Her heart pounded crazily as her lips moved helplessly under his and began to burn with a strange kind of fire.

When his mouth eased she would have wrenched herself free, but he shook his head, his mouth parting in a slight smile as he watched the dazed disbelief in her eyes. 'Not yet.'

Alex shivered and stiffened as his hand slid caressingly over her shoulders to her nape, to tangle in her soft thick hair. Gently he tugged her head back until the light from the stars shone directly into her shimmering, apprehensive eyes, illuminating her perfect satiny skin. She moaned softly and he pressed his thumb under her chin so she had to look at him.

Slowly he said, 'I suspected you were a little innocent, but I didn't know how much. I don't believe you've even been kissed properly before.'

Fright overtook her as this invasion of her privacy seemed unbearable. For the first time a man was delving at her innermost secrets and she found she couldn't endure it. She had been kissed before, but not like this, it was true. At least no one had ever made her feel as she did now, her pulse racing, her senses, always so cool, on fire.

'Please,' she whispered, not knowing how to fight

him but aware she must. 'We're strangers! I don't have
to answer questions like that.'

'We could never be strangers after this,' said Chase a
little angrily, his eyes on her own until she felt lost in his
compelling gaze. 'Couldn't you stop worrying and
relax? I'm not going to hurt you. I may have to one
day, but not yet. Another kiss won't harm you, I promise you that.'

'No . . .'

Again he bent his head and found her lips. Again his
mouth hardened more than it might have done as, once
more, she tried to push him away. She felt his mouth
punishing her futile endeavours to be free of him. He
swept away her resistance, like the onslaught of a flood
against which she had no means of saving herself. Yet
she knew it wasn't so much Chase she wanted to escape
as the blaze of excitement he was arousing inside her,
an excitement which made her want to cling to him and
forget all about tomorrow.

When he released her, her mouth was throbbing and
alive and she didn't want to leave him. She would have
liked to have pressed her face against his, to have
turned her burning lips against the coolness of his
cheek. She had to draw breath several times, in tormented little jerks, before she could speak. 'Are you
content now? You set out to frighten me.'

'I didn't set out to frighten you, at all. You know
that's nonsense! If anyone's frightened, it could be me,'
he exclaimed grimly, looking very like a man who had
fallen an unwilling victim to something that he had
realised, too late, was stronger than himself. He looked
down on her, unmoved by the glisten of tears in her
eyes, apparently more concerned with his own problems
than hers.

Incredibly all she could think of was the ecstasy she
had found in his arms. It remained so intense she had to
deny it. 'If you believe I enjoyed being half mauled,

you'd better think again!' she cried. 'It's not an experience I'd care to repeat.'

'You little liar!' he snapped softly. 'Next time I'll make you eat your words. You may be innocent, but you're not totally ignorant!'

Her mouth pursed with very young outrage, stung by his male arrogance. 'You've no right to talk to me like that!'

In control of himself again, he countered suavely, 'I think it's time someone took you in hand and showed you this other side to your nature. Consider it all part of growing up.' His eyes glinted. 'You've been well taught, well groomed, in some ways, by someone with some specific object in view, but sadly neglected in others.'

Thinking immediately of her mother, Alex started and shivered.

'I thought so.' There was satisfaction in his voice. 'Maybe tomorrow you might feel like telling me about it, but not now. You've had a long day with a lot packed into it and you might have to face an even longer one tomorrow. Run along in, Alex, and don't forget to say goodnight to Aunt Harriet on your way to bed.'

The next morning brought surprising news if nothing else. Alex hadn't closed her eyes until dawn and then she overslept. The others were having breakfast when she got down after a quick shower and dressing hastily in a pair of cotton jeans and thin top.

'I'm sorry I'm late,' she apologised.

Chase said nothing. As he rose to his feet and pulled out a chair for her she couldn't tell what he was thinking. His grey eyes watched her without giving anything away, yet as his glance touched her face he looked terribly alert, as though he was able to assess, without being told, exactly how long she had spent thinking about him through the night.

'Thank you,' she murmured as she sat down.

Henry was smiling over the table at her. 'You can be one of the first to congratulate me, Miss Latham—Alex. Ruby has agreed to marry me. Chase says you'll be staying for the wedding.'

Though Alex felt somewhat confused, she managed to convey to the happy pair that she was delighted. The engagement had happened so smoothly and quietly that she was beginning to wonder what all the fuss had been about. As for staying for the wedding, she would never do that, but this didn't seem the best time to refuse.

When she asked a radiant Ruby if her aunt knew of her engagement yet, Ruby nodded. 'We told her last night when we came in. Aunt Harriet's very pleased.'

Chase confused her even more by drawing up another chair, instead of returning to his place at the top of the table. Ignoring Ruby's raised eyebrows, he sat down beside Alex, practically touching her, pouring her a cup of hot coffee, then filling one for himself. Feeling her cheeks colour as he stared at her profile, she wished he would go away. She couldn't think why he took such pleasure in embarrassing her.

Henry had spent the night at Coolabra but was leaving that morning, taking Ruby with him to visit his parents. Alex was to go with them. It was all arranged, and she glanced at Chase in dismay. How much more had been decided on without consulting her? She didn't want to go anywhere, other than back to Melbourne! 'I've only just arrived here,' she was forced to protest. 'I've seen nothing of Coolabra yet.'

'You'll have plenty of time for that,' he assured her, turning to Henry, command in his voice, 'I'll bring Alex myself, this afternoon. You can go ahead with Ruby.'

Ruby looked startled. 'Alex can come with us, Chase. There's no need to put yourself out.'

'I'm sure Henry's parents won't mind putting me up,' Chase smiled sardonically. 'Alex and I will return tomorrow some time.'

He spoke to Alex next. 'Do you ride?'

Recovering her breath, she said yes. 'But I'm not very experienced.' She blinked at him, still slightly bemused by the speed at which everything seemed to be going. She was beginning to feel like a child on a fast round-about in a fairground, nervously longing for it to stop before she got completely dizzy. Henry Brett, a man a few years older than Ruby, was pleasant enough, and for Ruby's sake Alex felt pleased about their engagement, but wasn't it only yesterday that Ruby had been moaning at even having to see Henry again? Now here she was engaged to him and looking as if it was all she had ever wanted!

Nebulously she wondered how much of the credit for Ruby's engagement could be put down to her brother. He had a genius for organisation that stood out a mile! It staggered her that no one thought of opposing him, but she admitted it mightn't be easy. She would liked to have done so herself, by refusing to go riding with him, if that was what he was asking, but was disconcertingly aware she hadn't the courage. Besides, she might not be able to. While ostensibly she was here as Ruby's friend, she was still working for the firm and, unfortunately, the firm appeared to be Chase Marshall!

'I've not been on a horse much for years,' she added quickly, hoping that if he did intend going out with her, this would put him off.

'Never mind, you'll soon get enough experience, if I have anything to do with it,' he assured her crisply. 'We'll see you this afternoon, then?' In the rather blank silence that fell, he took Alex's arm and steered her firmly out into the hall.

'You'll need a hat,' he eyed her pale head decisively, 'otherwise that beautiful complexion will suffer, and I don't want that.'

A sharp retort sprang to her lips, but she never uttered it. With his eyes so steadily on her she found she could not. Instead she said obediently, 'I have one upstairs.'

'Good.' Just one word, but the crisp authority continued and she was helpless against it.

As he stood still, apparently to wait for her, she said hesitantly, 'Isn't there anything I can do, Chase? In the office, perhaps? You're paying me and I've always wanted to work in a station office. I can't just idle away my time.'

'You can't work here, not at the moment,' he replied impatiently. 'If you did, you'd soon arouse suspicion. But don't worry,' he smiled slightly into her anxious eyes, 'there'll be plenty to keep you fully occupied soon. Now run and fetch your hat.'

Over an hour later, when they turned to trot back to the homestead, Alex's face was full of delight. Joy bubbled inside her as everything she saw aroused a pleasure she found well nigh impossible to suppress. The station lay on the Georgina river, generally referred to as the Georgina, and named after the wife of a Queensland governor. Most of Coolabra lay in the northern Channel Country, but some of it spilled over into the Barkly Tablelands. The nearest town was the mining town of Mount Isa. The School of the Air was centred there, while Cloncurry, though further away, was the nearest Flying Doctor service.

Waterholes, left by the floods as they receded, were a major feature of the Channel Country. Chase told her they could stretch for up to twenty miles or more and be forty feet deep. He took her to one which, though not as big as this, was impressive. Alex's eyes widened on the huge expanse of water lined with river gum, coolabah and gidgee. Numerous birds flew up as they approached while others took little notice. She saw ibis, a wading bird with a curved bill, alongside ducks, herons, swans and egrets and countless others.

'It's amazing!' Alex exclaimed, unable to contain herself. 'So many birds, and everything so colourful. It's just as if an artist had run amok with his paintbrush. I've never seen anything like it!'

Chase smiled appreciatively. 'That's one way of putting it, but you express yourself nicely. I couldn't have done better.'

Unaccustomed to riding, she felt hot and looked at the water longingly. 'I'd love a swim,' she said ruefully, 'but I haven't brought anything.'

'You could always bathe nude,' he teased, knowing she would blush. 'Many's the time I have, especially when I was a boy. There's nothing quite like it.'

She could imagine! She would liked to have tried. Firmly she put a quick rein on thoughts which already had her floating sensuously out of her depth, Chase by her side. With a haste that betrayed her she changed to a safer subject, to steady her pulse.

The whole morning had been a kind of revelation to her, from the moment one of the hands had caught and saddled a beautiful little thoroughbred mare. Coolabra might be isolated, in so much as it was almost two hundred miles from another homestead, but the constant movement about the buildings and yards made it hard to believe in the station's isolation. Chase had shown her around the whole of it before they left and she had enjoyed the conducted tour so much she had quickly forgotten her former animosity. She had seen the stores, the office, the quarters for the staff men. The laundries, kitchens and cool-rooms—the stockyards and stables. It had been a tour of some magnitude and she suspected she had asked too many eager questions, but it was one she would never forget. Chase stayed by her side, often holding her arm to control her young enthusiasm, which was apt to run away with her, or just helping her over a rough piece of ground. With a patience she hadn't previously attributed him with, he answered all her queries and explained a lot more. It was a wonder there had been enough time left to come out here.

Away from the homestead the plains rolled endlessly, criss-crossed by the narrow channels from which this huge area of country took its name. Parts of this Channel Country, Chase remarked, when she told him her father was interested in grassland, could be more intensively developed for the beef industry. The pastures held their nutritional value for up to eight to ten months after rain. The spinifex, growing in wide clumps, would fatten cattle in drought, when there was nothing else, but it was the plants which sprang up quickly after watering that gave the area its reputation for turning off prime beef.

'I think you've had enough for your first morning,' he glanced at her glowing cheeks. 'You don't look exhausted, but I want you to enjoy the rest of the day. If we go much farther you might not, and I want to spend an hour in the office.'

'Yes, Chase,' she agreed, sure there was nothing else she could say. He had shown her a lot, she couldn't take up more of his time.

His mouth quirked. 'How deceptively meek you seem when you speak like that! You sound like a girl used to doing what she's told.'

'At home I suppose I am.'

He rode nearer, so that his leg brushed hers gently as the horses moved together. 'Your mother?'

Silently she nodded, a world of understated tension in her face. Without realising it some of her bright vitality faded as her eyes clouded. 'In a way . . .' she admitted.

'What's the trouble, exactly?' Casually he leaned towards her, cleverly finding just the right note to win her confidence.

Alex decided she could trust him. Perhaps, as a stranger, he might be safer than most to tell about her mother. He seemed to have guessed, anyway, and it might be a relief to mention it to someone. She needn't say much. She could make a joke of it to deceive him.

For most people it would be a joke! 'She would like to see me married to a millionaire.'

'Why not?' he drawled. 'You're lovely enough.'

She wished she hadn't told him. 'You're laughing at me!' she accused bitterly.

He sighed. 'I wish I were. I take it your mother is ambitious, Alex. Unfortunately there aren't that many millionaires around.'

Swallowing hard, she retorted, 'I'm only joking about a millionaire, of course. I suppose any man with a lot of money would do—for Mother.'

'But not for you? I take it you aren't very keen on the idea?'

'Don't be silly,' she forced a light smile, 'I can't see myself with anyone like that. A man with a quite ordinary income would satisfy me—if I loved him.'

'I see.' She had tried to lighten the atmosphere with a smile, but he didn't appear to be responding. His features seemed suddenly to tighten, although his voice remained laconic. 'Has she anyone specific in mind?'

'One or two . . .'

'So that's why you fled from Sydney?'

'Not particularly,' she hedged, knowing he didn't believe her for a moment. His brow had darkened formidably, his eyes narrowing characteristically. 'I went to Melbourne,' she explained, 'while my mother was in England. I just thought we needed a break from each other.'

'Hasn't she caught up with you yet?' he asked, catching hold of her rein to pull her horse to a standstill, as if her answer was important to him. He held her gaze with his own, refusing to let her look away. 'Answer me, Alex. Has she? Does she know where you are?'

'She thinks I'm up north, working. You don't have to get angry about it. I couldn't very well explain all this business about Ruby, could I?'

'I still don't feel I've got anywhere near the real

truth,' he snapped, between his teeth. For a moment he looked dangerous, ready to drag the truth violently out of her. The brilliant eyes he lowered over her seemed to lance right through her.

In panic Alex lost her usual cool self-possession. Without thinking she jerked her reins too fiercely from his hands. The horse she rode, being young and fairly highly strung, didn't appreciate this kind of treatment. Sharply she reared and bounded forward, her fine hooves kicking wildly up behind her as she flung Alex in a beautiful arch, right over her head.

The ground Alex landed on was hard. Momentarily she saw stars. Which must be crazy, she assured herself hazily, as she had fallen on her face. Her hands clenched, her fingers curling desperately around some coarse grasses. Then giving in to a great swirling weakness, she closed her eyes helplessly against the further punishment which she felt instinctively was about to descend on her already suffering head.

CHAPTER FIVE

ALEX lay quite still, in a pathetic heap, the breath knocked out of her. It wasn't the first time she had taken a fall from a horse, but it was the first time she had done anything quite so foolish. She had asked for all she got. She kept her eyes closed, not just because she was winded, but because she couldn't bear to see the contempt on Chase Marshall's face when he looked at her. He would be no admirer of anyone who treated a horse's mouth as roughly as she had done. She lay without moving. Almost immediately he was beside her.

'Alex?' She heard a roughness in his voice that suggested he was shaken. Touching her carefully, he turned her gently over, his hands sliding expertly over her limp body, feeling for broken bones. He muttered something she couldn't make out, but he sounded oddly distraught.

Ashamed of her cowardice, she made herself open her eyes. She smiled at him, so he would know she was all right as she tried to find her voice.

'I'm not hurt. See . . .' She moved her arms and slender legs, showing him.

'Why, you stupid little fool!' Now he was enraged, his eyes leaping in his pale face. 'Had you no more sense? You could have killed yourself!'

'Hardly,' she began, then broke off, her eyes pleading, trying to soothe him, 'I'm sorry . . .'

'Sorry!' Suddenly, as if he could express his disgust no other way, he bent his head, his mouth crushing hers.

If the fall had stunned her this was worse. Last night he had been comparatively gentle, now he was savage,

ridding himself of his frustration through the pressure
of his mouth.

She hated it, the pain he aroused, and held herself
rigid. 'Give,' he said thickly, something suddenly in his
eyes that sent shock waves shooting right through her.
She had never seen that in a man's eyes before, and
panic hit her, stronger than the other emotions he awak-
ened.

'Let me go!' she gasped, struggling against the tightening of his arms as he lowered himself to the grass
beside her. The grass, dried by the summer heat,
crackled and was still.

His mouth hesitated. He took it slowly from hers,
lifting himself away from her. Her heart stopped going
frantic in her breast.

'I'm sorry,' she scrambled to her feet. 'It was silly of
me to frighten my horse like that. I just wasn't thinking.'

'You should learn to control your temper. You're
like a child!'

His eyes narrowed. Alex could see he was still feeling
violent about something. Anxiously searching, she
stared up at him. In his face she could see anger, but
that peculiar lustful expression had gone. It had frightened her, though, and she wished she could forget it.

Another moment and Chase's anger faded too. He
turned to the horses, calmly grazing a few yards away.
'Let's get home.' He spoke abruptly, lifting her on to
the filly's back.

After lunch she flew with him to visit the Brett
station. 'Can you spare the time?' she asked.

'If I couldn't I wouldn't,' he said flatly. 'Drew Blake's
a good manager. He wouldn't be here if he couldn't get
along without me, and I'm away a lot.'

Alex considered her hands, relaxing their tightness.
Chase didn't give much away, but he sounded friendlier
than he had done an hour ago. He might have forgiven

her. Unhappy with her thoughts, she went on talking. 'Could you ever give up most of your other interests to live here permanently?'

'If I get married I will.'

Smiling, she said, 'Wouldn't you have to ask if she was prepared to live on an Outback cattle station before you proposed?'

'I fancy she would be willing to live anywhere with me.' His mouth quirked as he threw her a glance. 'How about you, Alex? Do you intend spending the rest of your life in an office? Your mother might be slightly misguided, but her ideas could be better than yours.'

'I like working, and office work needn't be dull.' She kept her smile pinned on. 'It doesn't represent every hour of my life. I have plenty of spare time.'

'Do you ever think of a husband and family?'

Thinking of Don Fisher, she rejected this immediately. 'I might, one day, but not for years yet.'

'Maybe I could change your mind.'

Quickly she looked at him, aware that he enjoyed teasing her. She had never seen Chase as her husband, but that couldn't be what he meant. 'You mean you're thinking of pointing out the advantages of marriage for a girl, to pass the time?'

'If it would help to convince you, someone might be grateful.'

So he was speaking generally. She should be relieved, but she knew a sharp hurting flicker of rejection. To hide it she laughed lightly. 'Was that all part of the plan, last night?'

He echoed her laughter, but his was much harsher. 'I don't think we plan those kind of interludes—but you were very responsive.'

The plane tipped a little. The sun was warm, the air slumbrous with heat and the dry arid scent of the plains below. Alex pushed back her heavy fair hair, feeling stifled. 'Can't you forget it?'

'I only forget what doesn't relate to the future,' he rejoined enigmatically.

'You can be sure I don't.' She shuddered as her eyes were drawn to his broad shoulders, the proud dark set of his head. 'I won't be here,' she said it in the manner of a prayer. 'Soon I'll be going home.'

'You won't be going anywhere for quite a while. Neither will I. I thought I'd already told you.'

Alex shrugged. It would be wonderful to stay here, a real experience, but she would have felt happier had Chase been planning to leave. When he was around she couldn't relax. Somehow he spelled danger. Obscurely she asked, 'If you stay at Coolabra, what about your girl-friend?'

'Girl-friend?' His voice was immediately cooler.

'The—the film actress. Ruby mentioned her.'

'Ah, Davina?'

'Not Davina Wilde?'

'The same,' he drawled, making no comment on the ring of awe in Alex's voice. 'But that's over.'

'How—how long did it last?'

Regretting having asked, since she expected to hear him telling her to shut up, Alex was surprised when he answered calmly, 'A few months. We parted on the best of terms.'

Sharply, it had been on the tip of her tongue to ask what terms Davina had demanded, but, horrified, she stopped herself in time, not knowing what possessed her. Chase would be a generous lover, probably he could afford to be. The lady of his choice wouldn't have to demand. Alex didn't know why the thought of Davina and him being lovers should make her go hot all over, but it did. A streak of something very like jealousy tore through her, and she was startled by it.

Coldly she said, 'I expect you're busy looking around for someone else?'

He turned his head, his eyes glinting, calculating the

heat in her cheeks. 'I'm no celibate, at my age, Alex. I've a normal male need of a woman, but I can do without.'

'I don't suppose your powers of resistance are very great,' she scoffed, remembering a certain look and recklessly returning frankness with frankness. 'Why don't you marry one of these women you sleep with?'

'Alex!' he groaned wryly. 'I haven't a harem, and if ever I made up my mind to marry whether we went to bed before or afterwards wouldn't be important.'

'But you wouldn't want a girl who'd been to bed with another man?'

'Oh, God . . . No, I would not!' suddenly he exploded with cold savagery. 'And don't start trotting out all that worn-out twaddle about what's sauce for the gander, etc. I've heard it all before and I'm not in the mood to listen.'

'Well!' she drew a deeply offended breath, 'I suppose a man like you thinks he's entitled to the best—that he can afford it?'

'You little vix . . .' Suddenly he stopped and laughed, brushing his hand around the back of his neck. 'Alex, please! Don't you think the conversation's getting a bit out of hand? We're going to help celebrate a happy occasion. We don't want to arrive looking as though we've been to a funeral—or battle!'

Alex was relieved when the Brett station came in sight. While she sat, apparently pale and subdued, inside she smouldered with resentment. Her resentment was not so much against Chase as fate. It was frightening to feel attracted to a man who found her boring, and whom she didn't even like!

Henry Brett was there to meet them and drove them quickly to the house. The homestead wasn't quite as grand as Coolabra but was extremely comfortable, all the same. Ruby was lucky, Alex decided. She would be well looked after here.

It turned out that Henry's parents were retiring to the original family station when Henry married. It was in New South Wales and much smaller than this one. They had only been waiting for Ruby and Henry to name the day. The surprising news about Ruby going off on holiday with another man had alarmed them, but now they could afford to laugh. It really was amusing that Alex had turned out to be a girl, a very attractive one at that! Alex being here certainly settled any lingering apprehension on that score. It was reassuring to know she was a friend of the Marshalls, from down south. According to Chase, who was never far from her side, she was going to be one of Ruby's bridesmaids. It certainly was going to be a wedding to remember!

Dinner that evening proved a very gay affair. They ate early and afterwards the lounge was crowded with neighbours dropping in to offer their congratulations to the happy pair. It wasn't, of course, the official engagement party. This would come later at Coolabra, Chase explained, and would take a few days to arrange. When people in the Outback had something to celebrate, they liked to make a good job of it.

It still astonished Alex that Ruby was so content after all her protesting in Melbourne. Now she was like a sleek, purring cat, replete after catching her quarry. She gave the impression she never wished to stray another inch from Henry's side.

There were more surprises in store, apart from Ruby. Startled, Alex glanced across the room to see a particularly beautiful woman coming through the door. This charming apparition was looking straight at Chase. Alex noticed the surprise on his face, but her own eyes were blank as he glanced at her sharply.

She was glad she had managed to appear indifferent as his gaze lingered on her for only a moment before returning to the new arrival. The woman made a beeline for him, after congratulating Ruby and Henry. Alex wasn't near enough to catch her name.

'Hello, darling! Aren't you pleased to see me?' As if in no doubt that he would be, the vision placed both hands on Chase's shoulders and kissed him warmly on the mouth. Nor did she hurry. Lightly he held her by the waist, kissing her back, giving every appearance of thoroughly enjoying himself.

'Oh, Chase!' the woman gushed, 'I have missed you. In fact I missed you so much, I took up Mary's invitation to visit. The play in New York folded up and it's three weeks yet before I start filming again.'

Alex went suddenly cold. This must be Chase's girlfriend? Ex-girl-friend, hadn't he said, but this woman was enticing enough to rekindle any man's interest. Seductively lovely and charming, she hung on Chase's arm, glowing up at him. Uncertainly, Alex turned away. Later she saw them talking closely together. Davina Wilde had her hand on Chase's muscular thigh, and she didn't keep it still. A peculiar sickness rose in Alex's throat. Davina was making no attempt to disguise what she was after!

When Chase went out, after midnight, to see Davina off, Alex slipped up to bed. Outside her bedroom door she met Ruby.

The other girl paused, her eyes sharp on Alex's pale face. 'I wondered why Chase wasn't in a hurry to get back to the big city. What do you think of Davina?'

Feeling she was being got at, Alex suggested evenly, 'He must have been surprised to see her.'

'I can't think why he should be.' Ruby smiled knowingly. 'It was all over the air this morning. I'm sure that's why he made it his business to be here.'

In her room, Alex found she was trembling, and hated Chase Marshall afresh that he could affect her like this. The feelings he had aroused in her so far hadn't been comfortable, but this sense of desolation was the worst yet. It made her all the more determined to escape as soon as she could.

The next day she returned with Chase to Coolabra

where preparations for the engagement party, proper, were already under way. Miss Marshall had everything under control, but was obviously in need of help. Alex, having spent the last hour or so enduring Chase's light but taunting conversation, was glad of the chance to forget it. Why should it matter to her what he had been up to the night before? Why should he be so interested in her reactions? The fact that she wasn't sophisticated enough to listen to his occasional remarks about women and sex without blushing had appeared to amuse him. Why, Alex wondered angrily, when he apparently had never done without sex himself, was he so dryly critical of the women who supplied it?

When Miss Marshall almost begged for her assistance, Alex was only too willing to give it. Anything would be better than just sitting around the house thinking of Chase, with a mind too eager to concentrate on his dark attraction! She threw herself at the task of helping Miss Marshall unstintedly, in order to alleviate the peculiar restlessness that invaded her. If Chase had set out deliberately to arouse dormant feelings, she decided bitterly, he shouldn't have the satisfaction of knowing how well he had succeeded.

'I hope you aren't wearing yourself out?' he said, when, a few nights before the party, he came across her by the pool. The swimming pool was beautiful, in keeping with everything else around the station homestead, but he eyed both it and Alex grimly. 'Should you be swimming alone when you're tired?'

Alex didn't see why not. She had just been in the pool and felt better for it. Glancing at the water, she saw it was still, and wished her heart would be, when he approached her. As she put her hand over it nervously, the beat quickened even more as his eyes rested on her uneasy fingers. She was aware, from the way his eyes glinted, that he knew very well what she was trying to hide.

Quickly she reached for her towelling jacket, uncaring that mockery now joined the interest in his gaze as she slipped into it. This accomplished, she sat back with what she hoped was dignity on the luxurious lounger where she had been lying. 'I am a little tired,' she admitted, 'but then so is everyone. All except you,' she added, resigned to his energy, which never diminished. She was just beginning to fully realise the strength of him. Coolabra and his other stations in the chain might have excellent managers, but he was the power behind them. Very definitely! Before, she had had a vague idea this was so, and the last few days had confirmed this irrefutably. Chase's was the word that carried. He ruled and overruled with ruthless authority, in absolute control of just about everything. The weather, she thought wryly, might be one of the few exceptions. And herself, she hoped!

Coolabra itself was a small empire, not so isolated in some ways as she had imagined. The office was an eye-opener. She had heard Chase dictating. Some of the more important members of his staff flew in and out regularly. He knew exactly what was going on everywhere. If he didn't it was a situation that was soon rectified. He had a cool command that she envied, even if it made him seem very often something less than human. She found Drew Blake and some of the other men much easier to be with.

Yes, these past few days had certainly opened her eyes! Flicking the damp hair back from her face, she wished they hadn't. Now her entire vision was filled by a man who unconsciously frightened her, his total strength seeming to reduce her feminine weakness to nothing.

The air was till warm. She loved this time of night, after dinner, with the heat of the day gone with the light but the stars overhead supplying sufficient to see by. This was only the second time she had bathed as normally she stayed in the drawing room with Miss Marshall and those members of the staff who joined them for dinner. This evening, for one reason or another, everyone had dispersed and Miss Marshall had gone to bed.

'I suppose it might be foolish of me to swim alone,' she said, when Chase didn't speak, 'but I haven't come to any harm.'

'You might have done.' His lancing glance penetrated the darkness. 'You look breakable. Are you eating properly?'

'Of course. I'm naturally thin.' Some water ran from her hair down her cheek and she brushed it off, looking around for something to dry it with. She found a handkerchief in her pocket.

'Where's your towel?' he asked.

She shrugged. 'I usually wring my hair out and dry off naturally.'

'Go ahead,' he said evenly. 'Don't mind me.'

Her heart began racing, knowing she did. Patiently, giving herself time to recover, she explained, 'I didn't do anything about my hair because I was going in again.'

'Fine.' Chase sounded amused, lazily so. 'I'll join you. No need to deny yourself the pleasure because I'm here. I feel like a swim myself.'

Turning, he disappeared into one of the changing rooms, leaving her frowning and hesitating. It was his pool. On those grounds alone she couldn't very well object, but she had no wish to share the intimacy of moonlight bathing with him. She would rather have kept the remainder of any time they must spend together on a more businesslike footing. Nor had she any particular desire to see him stripped, as he had been when they had swum off the beach in Victoria.

An idea came to her suddenly. Quickly she slipped out of her jacket and slid into the pool. Like a slender fish, she swam silently to the other side, coming up where the branches of an overhanging tree cast protec-

tive shadows. Here she would wait until Chase entered
the water, then she could immediately climb out. That
way he need never guess she was nervous of being alone
with him. She was sure it was nervousness, the feeling
which had never left her since she had fallen from her
horse and he had kissed her.

The rustling silence mocked her as the night breeze
moved through the branches of the trees. A bird
chirped above her head, so near she was startled, and
unconsciously she reacted, tossing back her star-silvered
hair, a habitual movement which must have betrayed
her. Before she could take another breath, Chase was
there. He had slipped around the back of the changing
rooms, reaching her side of the pool while she had been
watching the other.

Her eyes widened in alarm as his feet touched
the pool bottom. Although the night was warm she
shivered.

'Your hair is distinctive,' he smiled down at her, 'like
a sheet of silver floating behind you. You could never
escape unnoticed in the dark with hair like that.'

Had he known what she was doing? She stared up at
him, seeing again the width of his bare shoulders. She
had seen him before like this, but it hadn't affected her
breathing as it did now.

'Come on,' he grinned, apparently unaware she was
shaking, 'what are we waiting for, my small water
nymph? You're a very good swimmer. I'll race you.'

The challenge, thrown with idle amusement, was one
she swiftly took up. Feeling safer, she nodded, striking
away from him to the other end of the pool. Chase
would win easily, but as soon as he passed her she
would leave him and scramble out. Unfortunately she
acted too soon. When he drew ahead by a couple of
lengths, she turned, but managed no more than a few
strokes in the opposite direction before he caught up
with her.

'Where do you think you're going?' he asked, his eyes glinting, as silver as her hair in the eerie half-light.

'Out!' She tried to speak lightly, hoping her obvious breathlessness would convince him she had had enough.

'Just because you weren't winning?' he laughed. 'You can't always, you know.'

'It's not that,' she was trying to decide the best way to get round him. 'I've been in long enough. I didn't think you would mind if I packed in before you did.'

'I mind.' His hands came out to catch her suddenly to him. 'Not about the race but being deprived of your company. How can we get to know each other better if you run off every time I try to get near you?'

'I don't,' she protested, while guiltily aware he might be speaking the truth. She did her best to avoid him, perhaps unconsciously, but hadn't guessed he had noticed.

'Yes, you do.' His voice altered. He sounded pre-occupied, playing with the strap of her bikini as though not aware of what he was doing. Lean and dark, he towered above her, the water dripping down his strong neck to glisten on the thick fuzz below. 'I'll have to make sure you aren't so inclined to run away in future.'

The threat in his voice was light, but she stiffened, receiving the impression that he wasn't simply amusing himself any more. He was like a man with an objective in view and, for reasons she didn't understand, deadly serious. When he wanted something badly he might let nothing stand in his way. 'You're joking, of course,' she breathed.

'Not where you're concerned. Not now.'

In nervous bewilderment, as she stared up at the stark lines of his face, she scarcely realised his hands had moved until the narrow straps were being pushed from her shoulders. As the brief bikini top slid down to her waist he pulled her swiftly against him.

'Chase!' she gasped, only to have her apprehensive protest smothered underneath his descending mouth.

His chest hurt her. It was rough against her bare skin and she had never been as close as this to a man before. She wanted to cry out, to struggle. She managed to do this until, as if ignitable fluid ran through her veins and he put a match to it, flames began searing mercilessly through her.

As he felt her half-naked body go limp, his mouth became more urgent, probing her parted lips sensuously. Helplessly, Alex seemed unable to prevent him. Shaping the back of her head, he held her quite still until she ceased struggling and began to respond. Before she could control them, her fingers traced a path up his broad back to bury themselves in the thickness of his dark hair.

With a smothered groan he lifted her in his arms, carrying her from the pool to the lounger. Laying her on it, he came down beside her, still holding her tightly. 'You're beautiful,' he muttered, staring at her. 'You have a beautiful body.'

Again he began kissing her, his mouth sliding over her face and throat, his hands curving her hips to the strength of his limbs, leaving her in no doubt of the urgency of his desire. Her senses swam as she wriggled in an attempt to draw away, which only seemed to incite him further.

'Alex,' he demanded thickly, 'have you ever belonged to a man?'

'No!' She was too dazed and incredibly excited to answer with anything but the truth. Chase overwhelmed her. She couldn't move or think.

'I want to marry you,' his voice was pitched low, but she heard, every syllable hitting her like shock. 'I want to give Coolabra a girl like you, someone untouched. Someone to give me the children I need.'

'Marry you?' Frightened indescribably, she went

rigid. 'For Coolabra?'

'That's what I said.' He took no notice of her wide startled eyes, his mouth turning to touch the inside of her arm as she withdrew it stiffly from around his neck. His movement was almost lazy. Obviously he considered the battle more than half won and didn't take her protesting too seriously. His mouth lingered on the sensitive area of skin, assessing the nerve beat, feeling her quiver. In another moment she would become fully alive, both to him and the honour he was bestowing.

Conscious of what he was thinking, she went cold. 'No, Chase. I can't think you mean it, but even if you did, I can't marry you.'

'You're confused.' He lifted his head, his lips near hers again, his voice teasing, his eyes intent. 'I haven't proposed to a girl before, Alex. You can feel flattered. Marry me and you'll have everything you ask for. So will your mother—a millionaire.'

'Don't be silly!' What was he talking about? Was he trying to impress? Did he think he could buy her? He wanted someone without blemish for Coolabra. For this he had made passionate love to her, a girl who, by the evidence of his own lips, bored him. All for his beloved station! She was amazed and sorry for him. It must have gone greatly against the grain having to come down from the elevated position he occupied to plead like this, to humble himself. If this really was what he was doing. More likely he believed in short cuts. A leisurely wooing would be beyond his patience when he wanted a girl for only one purpose. He was treating her as he would any woman, convinced he had merely to arouse her to render her incapable of resisting him—It wasn't easy to! Alex felt a wave of bitterness against her own too responsive body. His lovemaking did turn her on. She wasn't so naïve that she wasn't up with most of the current expressions, but love didn't come into it. Desire could generate a burning heat in the blood, but how long did it last without love to support it?

'No, Chase,' she tried to push him away, to speak firmly. 'If you're serious about wanting to marry me then I have to refuse.'

His eyes narrowed consideringly on her flushed but oddly determined face. 'Darling child,' he mocked, 'do you realise what you're turning down?'

'Now you're being insulting!' She struggled so fiercely he let her go. Embarrassed to distraction, she fumbled to cover herself with her bikini. Her fingers trembled so much it took her ages to fix it and then put on her short robe. Chase didn't offer to help, but sat and watched until she could have screamed. 'You're insulting!' she contented herself by repeating.

'I heard the first time.' His tolerance was converted to anger that made a glitter of his eyes through the darkness. 'Find me one woman who would agree with you. God, I've asked you to marry me, Alex, not go to bed with me, at least not until after the ceremony. Why, I haven't even tried to make love to you properly, and I'm willing to bet you'd be a hot little thing, once the first time was over. I couldn't think of anyone who would deny you'd been honoured. I've paid you a compliment you might not receive again.'

Equally angry, Alex exclaimed, 'You want to marry me, but you don't love me. You only want me for—for breeding purposes. It's—it's disgusting!'

'Love!' His strongly fashioned mouth curled back in a mirthless smile. 'If you're waiting for love you might never get a ring on your finger. Come to that,' his eyes glinted derisively, 'do you love me?'

'No, but I wasn't the one who did the proposing!'

'Understood,' he scoffed insolently. 'And love disposed of. So what's left to worry about? Your mother?'

'No!' Alex was too agitated to know what she was saying. 'She would approve of you, all right. She'd think me a fool not to take you. But as she's not here she can't force me. This is one time I don't have to run—when I can make up my own mind.'

The thoughtful flash in his eyes passed as she jumped to her feet, his hand automatically going out to help her. Very slightly he smiled. 'I can wait, but I won't promise not to try and wear you down. You'll soon find out I can be pretty potent, when I put my mind to it. We could be married before Ruby.'

'No, Chase!' She shivered. Mistaking it for cold, she huddled tighter in her robe, her eyes veiled. 'I don't want you wasting your time over me. I won't ever marry—I've had it rammed down my throat far too often.'

'You're crazy, girl.' His hard voice was clipped. 'I'm not just any man.'

'Not so crazy as you're bigheaded!' she whispered vehemently. 'Look, my mother exhausts herself trying to push me into marriage, and now you! I don't want it. I have my own life to lead. Can't you believe it?'

'I believe you believe it, but I'm not convinced,' he taunted, a belief in his own power dominating his dark face. 'From now on you can take it you're being pursued, and you can certainly believe that! My patience is not unlimited. I can't guarantee I'll fight clean, either, but I do have the decency to give you fair warning.'

In the darkness Alex was all pale contours, very slight, suddenly beset by a terrible exhaustion, particularly of the spirit. How could she fight him, if he meant what he said? She wanted to be free, unchained. Any invisible threads she felt holding her to this man must be easily breakable. In his arms she felt imprisoned, committed, imperilled by her own passion as much as his. A few minutes ago she had been burning up like a fire, driven by forces she could no more control than understand. It disturbed the even tenor of her life just to be near him. Marriage was clearly impossible!

'I must go in,' she said quietly, the note of finality bringing his head up sharply.

He went suddenly still, but the darkness, the forcefulness of him halted her in her tracks, not to be ignored. 'Alex! You'd better give yourself time to think it over. Consider the advantages. You'd have everything money could buy. In return all I ask is your help in entertaining. I do a lot and I'll be badly in need of a hostess now that Ruby's getting married and my aunt too old. The only other thing I ask of you is children, and I haven't wanted them with any other woman before.'

Chase Marshall's children? Her nerves contracting deep in her stomach, her mouth suddenly dry, Alex looked at him, her cheeks burning. 'Why don't you ask Miss Wilde? I'm sure she would give you beautiful children.'

The set of his head was answer enough. 'I'm proposing to you, not Miss Wilde. I suggest you concentrate on that.'

'My answer will still be the same,' she replied, in a kind of frantic panic leaving him to skim the dewy lawns to the house. She thought it was his footsteps following until she realised it was the wildly pounding beat of her own heart.

The next day Chase was going to Mount Isa. Alex learnt this over breakfast and the tension that had gripped her all night lessened as she contemplated a whole day without him. Her relief was shortlived. It turned to despair when Aunt Harriet produced a shopping list and begged Alex to go with him. It was mostly extra stuff they needed for the party. She would be eternally grateful if Alex would go.

As Miss Marshall rushed out again to consult with Mrs Young, Chase looked up from a personal letter the mail plane had just brought in. 'You aren't thinking of refusing?'

'I don't see how I can,' she retorted sharply, feeling trapped. Chase had behaved over breakfast exactly the same as usual, but she wasn't altogether reassured. Somehow she didn't trust him.

He was studying her face slowly, no doubt taking the credit for the dark shadows under her eyes. They betrayed her sleepless night, which he had obviously and arrogantly decided was because of him.

'You could get yourself a new dress for the party. Mount Isa has fine shops.'

'I have one that will do nicely,' she answered, looking away from him.

'Let me buy you another. I'll come with you, if you like.'

'A fine lot of talk that would cause! No, thank you.'

'But you're still coming?'

'Do I have any other choice?' She stared at him coldly, feeling miserable without knowing why.

'You have a rare gift for enthusiasm,' he remarked cuttingly. 'Or is it only me?'

'We were talking of a trip to town.'

'Were we?'

They stared at each other like two antagonists, until Alex's eyes fell before his indisputable authority. 'Don't lose any more sleep about it,' he drawled, getting lithely to his feet. 'Both the trip and my company might be better for you than you think. Be ready in half an hour.'

CHAPTER SIX

MOUNT ISA, on the banks of the Leichhardt, was the most important industrial, commercial and administrative town in north-western Queensland. Its copper and lead fields were well known, as was the living standards and modern amenities provided for the men and their families who worked there. Alex had heard that along with good housing there was a large variety of leisure facilities to choose from—a golf course, tennis courts, a ten-pin bowling alley, water-skiing and sailing, to name but a few. Apart from these there were churches and schools, including a technical college, and the town had well stocked shops.

Chase told her Mount Isa attracted a lot of tourists who wanted to see something of the real Australia. In the winter, he said, there was a large rodeo, usually a two-day event, which brought rough-riders from all over the State.

'I'll take you,' he glanced at her coolly as the plane landed and came to a standstill on the runway. His mouth quirked. 'As my wife you'd be entitled to my company.'

'On the rare occasions you were home?' Alex observed sharply, averting her eyes.

'Does that mean you've decided to marry me?'

'No, it does not!' Her voice wasn't quite steady enough, but she felt her meaning was clear.

This appeared to have little effect on his confidence. He smiled, as if likening her to a fly attempting to escape from a web. 'I intend being home most of the time, if that's what's worrying you.'

'You did say you wanted a family.' Her cheeks

flushed as she replied with an audacity she had never
dreamt herself capable of. 'I suppose that would take
time.'

'Do you?' he replied, so softly that she immediately
regretted mentioning it. Why could he so easily embarrass her, provoke her into saying all the wrong things?

'What time are we leaving?' she asked quickly, glancing at him mutinously out of her vivid blue eyes.

'After lunch.' His black brows tilted. 'I take it you'll
be willing to share that with me?'

Ignoring his sarcasm, she nodded, listening carefully
as he gave her detailed instructions as to where he
would meet her. 'I'll be there,' she promised lightly, deliberately indifferent as she left him.

Later that morning, as she walked around a corner,
Alex saw him talking to Davina Wilde. Davina had her
hand on his arm, so that the rest of her was very close
to him and she was smiling. Chase looked down at her
and he, too, was smiling. Alex, pausing uncertainly,
noticed his hand go out to touch the film star's cheek.

Angrily Alex turned in the opposite direction, feeling
slightly sick. Not because Chase and Davina were together—it was simply a question of deploring bad taste.
How could a man propose to one girl and flirt so blatantly with another? It just proved, she thought bitterly,
that regarding herself, Chase had no deep feelings whatsoever!

As they ate a very good lunch in the hotel later, he
asked Alex if she had enjoyed her shopping.

'Yes,' she answered, meeting the silvery intentness in
his eyes. 'I saw you did, too.'

'Meaning?'

'I saw you with Miss Wilde.' She hadn't intended
mentioning it, but her tongue ran away with her. Why
had she let it? Surely he was free to talk to anyone he
liked?

He asked, with a kind of lazy amusement, 'Were you
jealous?'

'No, why should I be?'

He placed a hand unexpectedly over hers and she went tense as needles of excitement pricked up her arm, causing a nerve to jerk at the corner of her mouth. Quickly she snatched her hand from under his. Panic flashed in her eyes and she could see he was drawing his own conclusions from it.

'Jealousy is a perfectly natural emotion, Alex, one we're all born with.' Sardonically he went on, 'Last night you turned down my proposal. Today you see me with another woman and you don't like it.'

'I didn't say that . . .'

'It bothered you, though. You even thought it contemptible.'

Alarmed by his astuteness, she gasped, 'I didn't say that, either!'

'When we're married——' Chase began suavely.

Suddenly she felt suffocated by his persistence, frightened by it. It made her wonder if she would ever find sufficient strength to fight him. 'I haven't agreed to marry you,' she hissed, 'so keep your voice down!'

'I never give up, Alex.' His mouth thinned and his eyes lost their tolerance. 'I told you last night I always get what I want, one way or another. Even if I have to use a little force.'

'You can't mean to kidnap me?' she challenged witheringly, her voice dismissing such a suggestion as absurd.

'Not unless all else fails,' he snapped, enjoying the quick quiver of fear she was unable to hide.

Ruby's engagement party was a huge success. Alex enjoyed it but found she was relieved when it was over. She liked Coolabra best when it was quiet, and after the party some of the guests had stayed for almost a week. She could see, though, what Chase meant about entertaining. Coolabra was ideally suited to it, with its big lounges and spacious bedrooms, many of which were en suite. Then, outside, there was riding, swimming and

tennis, or just lounging with drinks on the wide ver-
andah or in the wonderful gardens. While on the more
serious side, if one was interested, and a lot were, there
was much to see of the work and skill involved in the
running of a large property. Wistfully, she thought of
her father. He would love it, as she did, Alex knew, as
his research was mostly agricultural.

During the party, and the days which followed,
Chase had been attentive, but not so much as to cause
undue speculation. He had danced more with Davina
and other equally scintillating ladies. Alex found herself
hoping, not without cause, that he had changed his
mind about marrying her.

So reassured was she by his continuing reserve, she
consented to stay and help with the wedding. As this
was to be at Coolabra there was certainly enough to do
and there was little doubt she was needed. It even went
to her head a little when both Miss Marshall and Mrs
Young assured her that for a nineteen-year-old girl her
efficiency was remarkable. In spite of all this, however,
Alex realised she had no alternative but to stay, as she
was virtually a prisoner.

Ruby, with her head in the clouds, was too busy gathering a trousseau together to be of much help with the
practical side of things. She was willing to gossip and
talk about her wedding, but that was all. Chase was
curiously withdrawn, busy most of the time in his office
or out on the station.

One day Ruby remarked on this. 'He was only going
to stay a few days. It's years since he's been here so
long. We're all surprised.'

'He couldn't very well leave on the eve of your
wedding,' Alex replied, without looking up from the
slip she was mending.

'I'm not so sure.' Ruby's eyes were frankly sceptical.
'Davina is still here and I can see she's still interested.
Maybe this is it? Has he said anything to you?'

'No.' Alex kept her reply brief and her head bent over her work. What would Ruby think of her brother's proposal? she wondered. Of course she might not believe it as, like Chase, she would never believe any girl in her right senses would turn him down.

Davina stayed for several more days after the other guests had departed, contributing nothing but perhaps her undoubted beauty. She rose at noon and spent the greater part of every afternoon by the pool. In the evenings she contrived to display almost as much of her body at dinner. She could wear the most outrageous dress and get away with it. Sometimes Alex almost blushed for her until she remembered the actress was used to the limelight and dressed to attract it to herself.

'I'm trying to imagine you in a gown like Davina's,' Chase teased Alex one evening as he handed her a dry sherry. 'My guess is you'd be even more spectacular.'

'I couldn't carry it off,' she answered stiffly, fixing her eyes on the glass of whisky he had poured for himself. She wished he would go and talk to someone else, but he stayed by her side.

'I might carry you off,' he muttered, 'if you were inside that.'

'Why don't you try such caveman tactics on Miss Wilde?' she suggested sharply.

'Ah, but Miss Wilde doesn't provoke me as you do,' he returned smoothly, his eyes on the neat little dress her mother had chosen. It didn't hide the full curves of her breasts but did little else for her. Tersely impatient of a sudden, he said, 'Your hair is wonderful, Alex, like pale silk. You've a skin like satin and nature couldn't improve much on your figure, but I'd like to get my hands on the person who chooses your clothes. Your mother?'

Colour flared in Alex's cheeks. The impulse to hit out at the insolence in his eyes had never been greater, but conscious that they weren't alone, she controlled herself. 'My clothes are good.'

'So's bread and butter.' His tone was dryly dismissive. 'When we're married . . .'

The booming of the gong mercifully interrupted, Polly, one of the Aborigine girls, using a heavy hand this evening. 'Allow me,' Chase murmured, grasping Alex's rigid arm firmly and leading her in to dinner.

Alex wasn't so angry that she didn't see how this surprised the others. In the dining room, as he released her, she felt it expedient to find some explanation for Aunt Harriet. His last words and actions disturbed her so much she mumbled the first thing to enter her head.

'I wanted to ask Chase about his horses. He has some beautiful thoroughbreds. Miss Wilde and I were watching Drew Blake exercising one after tea. We were just saying how we rarely get the opportunity of seeing them.'

She hadn't counted on Chase overhearing. She didn't know he had until she heard him saying suavely, with the hidden intention to punish,

'I'll take you on a conducted tour in the morning, darling, if you're up soon enough.'

Mischievously, driven by a devil, Alex smiled at Davina, who was sitting beside her. 'I think Mr Marshall must be speaking to you, Miss Wilde?'

Davina, more than willing to believe it, looked back at Alex, her eyes sparkling with triumph. 'Do you know, it's an invitation I've been angling for ever since I came, but Chase is so difficult to pin down.' Radiantly she smiled at him, perhaps mistaking a flicker of vengeful fury for pleasure. 'You are the oddest man, darling. You do choose your time to tell me!'

Alex couldn't understand why her heart was so heavy next morning when she saw them going off together. Last night, ignoring Chase's grim expression, she had congratulated herself on outsmarting him. This morning she wasn't so sure. She would have loved to have gone riding with him. Reluctantly she confessed it. The thought of Davina sharing with him all the early morning freshness reduced the triumph she had felt to nothing. It was being rapidly replaced by a growing uncertainty, a conviction, not easily dispelled, that she didn't fully realise what she was up against. Chase hadn't approached her after dinner. He sat in the lounge drinking whisky instead of coffee, talking to the others, but somehow this had aroused in Alex only a fresh and terrible uneasiness.

Making a great effort, she closed her eyes to the sight of his tall, well made figure disappearing in the distance and turned back to the house. Goodness knows, there was plenty to do, and if she was tired enough she could have no energy left for thinking.

Ruby paused by her on her way to the pool. 'Why don't you join me, Alex?' she asked. 'Aunt Harriet's still in bed. She won't want you for at least another hour and I see Chase has gone off with Davina. I believe they're riding out to the mustering camp, though what Davina will do there I can't think. Anyway, they probably won't be back until later in the day, so he won't want you either.'

Alex hesitated, sorely tempted but conscientiously resolute. 'I promised I'd have a batch of letters ready for your aunt's signature. Also some for your brother which I didn't manage to finish yesterday. I'm not on holiday now, you know.'

Ruby didn't look too perturbed about that. 'Well, don't make it sound like a penance, young Alex. Staying here can't be worse than sitting in a mouldy old office in Melbourne. And think of all the fun of an Outback wedding. It's a chance you might never get again.'

'I didn't want to come here in the first place, remember?' She thought Ruby could have remembered a lot of things she apparently found it more convenient to forget. A few short weeks ago it was Coolabra that had been 'mouldy'.

Not at all put out, Ruby shrugged. 'Never mind. Stop worrying! Your visit has certainly served its purpose. Henry is quite convinced he jumped to the wrong conclusions. What do you think?'

'It's not really any of my business, is it?' Alex refused to be drawn. She had no idea what Henry Brett believed, but he must be able to work a lot out for himself. He wasn't a stupid man and if he was satisfied surely that was all that mattered. Ruby might be better advised to leave things alone. Ruby considered she had hoodwinked Henry, but mightn't she be the one who was being fooled? Henry wanted her, all right, but once married he would be master of his own household, Alex was sure of that. What bothered her, at the moment, was her own inability to get away from Coolabra. She wished Ruby might give some thought to that!

Wondering if she could appeal to her, Alex was startled to hear Ruby exclaim, 'Wouldn't it be fun if we were to have a double wedding? Chase and Davina! It's just occurred to me. Would you say they were in love?'

'They've only gone riding,' Alex faltered, again avoiding a direct reply.

'I don't know,' Ruby frowned. 'Chase was keen enough a few weeks ago, but it sort of fizzled out. He didn't follow her to Sydney, he came to Melbourne instead.'

'To investigate you,' Alex reminded her.

'Yes, but I still can't make it out. Davina's at Coolabra—which must mean something, and Chase hasn't gone away. And my wedding isn't responsible. He would never let it get in the way of business. There has to be another reason why he stays, and both Aunt Harriet and I think it can only be Davina.'

In the office, which she reached eventually, Alex tried to compose herself. If Chase had fallen in love, which she doubted, after his remarks on the subject by the pool, she hoped it was with Davina. She couldn't understand why even contemplating this should make her feel slightly ill, but her own feelings for him were so confused she couldn't even begin to sort them out. He could make her heart race and her hands go clammy, but somehow, she was coming to associate him too much with her mother. They both appeared to have the same ambition to see her married. While the two had never met, their characters merged continually in Alex's head. They both thought marriage should be a girl's sole goal, that, willy-nilly, she should be pushed into it. Neither of them, she felt sure, would ever stop to consider what the girl herself wanted.

Davina and Chase returned to the homestead during the afternoon and, to everyone's surprise, Davina left the station an hour later. No one said anything. Davina's coldly angry face seemed sufficient explanation. She wasn't even coming back for the wedding.

'Which proves how wrong I was to be talking of a double one!' Ruby whispered dryly to Alex as she went to get ready to spend the evening with Henry. 'Do you think Chase overheard?'

'They might make it up. I mean, if they've merely fallen out,' Alex added hastily.

'I doubt it,' carelessly Ruby shook her head. 'I recognise the death of hope on any girl's face. Chase can be a brute when he wants to be.'

The house seemed quiet with Davina gone, but Alex liked it better. Henry arrived to collect his fiancée. They had been asked to dine with some friends of his in Mount Isa. Ruby would sleep at the Brett station where tomorrow she would discuss last-minute wedding plans with Henry and his parents.

After dinner Aunt Harriet announced she was having an early night and Chase asked Alex to come to his study. 'I want to speak to you,' he said curtly.

She was tired. They were all tired, having spent one of those kind of endless days that come before a wedding. There was so much to do. As fast as one job was completed there was another two to take its place. At dinner, Alex could see Aunt Harriet was looking exhausted. While she was in the study with Chase she must mention it. It would be an opportunity.

She wore a long-skirted dress in pink, with a demure neckline. She had had it since she was seventeen, and while she knew the colour was a bit unfashionable it was a dress she was fond of. It had been an effort to change at all, this evening, but she was familiar enough with Coolabra now to know it would be regarded as almost a sin not to. Here everything stopped for dinner, and guests and family alike were expected to dress accordingly.

'Come in,' said Chase, when she knocked.

Alex did so and closed the door. Tall and darkly handsome, in his well cut clothes, he seemed to envelop and tower over her. Her breath catching in her throat, she stared at him, looking very fragile and far more appealing than she knew. Her hair fell, fair and softly shining, on either side of her perfectly modelled face, and her eyes, deeply blue, held an oddly trapped expression. She broke into speech with a haste that reflected her nervous state of mind.

'Your aunt is exhausted, Chase. I think you should insist she has a day in bed.'

'My dear girl,' he grated, 'do shut up and sit down. My aunt will probably agree to spending a month in bed, after the wedding. But before that, never. She may be tired out, but she's the only one who's supposed to know it.'

Alex gritted her teeth. 'You understand, I hope, that she could collapse?'

'No, she won't. And we must see she doesn't—unobtrusively, I mean.'

'I'll do what I can,' Alex agreed fretfully.

'Only three more days. They'll go in a flash.'

Bitterly she nodded. 'I do hope you're right. I don't

think I could stay here much longer. Oh,' against Chase's raised eyebrows, she threw out her hands, 'I realise I couldn't abandon Miss Harriet now, but it all seems so pointless.'

'Of course it isn't,' he said crisply, pouring her a sherry and helping himself to whisky. 'It's good training for your own wedding, which will soon follow.'

Too weary to fight him, she sighed, half closing her eyes. He might have passed a casual remark, but she didn't think so. He had a very purposeful look in his eye and she couldn't fight his immense vitality. Tonight she couldn't even try. Deliberately she made light of it, pretending it was a joke. 'I think Ruby's wedding will be enough to last me a lifetime. Who would want to go through all this again?'

'Unfortunately,' he observed coolly, 'unless you want to live in sin, as I'm sure your mother would still term it, there's no other way.'

'I suppose not.' Delicately Alex yawned, while her small feet edged warily towards the door. 'But as I'm not thinking of marrying or living in sin, why should I worry?'

'Where do you think you're going?' he asked harshly. 'I told you to sit down.'

She came back to him, not wishing to be thought a coward but desperately reluctant to remain. Why hadn't she thought of an excuse and gone to bed, like Miss Harriet? 'I finished all your mail,' she pleaded. 'Was that what you wanted to see me about?'

'Mail?' He might never have known there was such a thing. 'No, it was not. I want to know if you've come to your senses about marrying me yet. You've had long enough to think it over. I won't announce our engagement on the day Ruby marries, but plenty of people will be staying over. It will be as good a time as any. Then, if you don't think you can face another big wedding, we can be married quietly within a few days.'

'You're mad!' She jumped back in alarm as she realised what he was saying. Her heart thumped in terror as he followed up, looming above her. 'Quite mad!' she exclaimed, her eyes wide on his hardening expression. 'No one would believe that you, of all people, would act this way. It's completely out of character.'

Derogatorily his eyes narrowed, and he didn't need to put in words just how dimwitted he considered any girl who refused such a bargain as himself! 'I'm not interested in what it is. Nor do I care desperately about other people's opinions. Most men act out of character at some time in their lives. It's sometimes necessary, especially when dealing with a featherbrained girl like you.'

Angrily she cried, 'Shouldn't you be congratulating yourself on a lucky escape? You surely couldn't do with a fool for a wife, one you don't even like! I don't like you much, either,' she ended sharply, refusing to admit that that might not be true.

Chase seized her wrist as she took another step backwards. 'Come here!' he said bitingly, jerking her tense body to him. 'If you have to be convinced that you're perfectly normal, under all those stiff and mysterious inhibitions, there are better ways of doing it than talking.'

'No, Chase!' She wasn't to be conquered this way! If he chose to use brute force to gain his own way, she would never submit without a struggle. 'Stop it!'

As her voice rose hysterically, so did her hand. It had been a purely defensive action, but she had forgotten the glass of sherry she held. She couldn't remember throwing it deliberately, but suddenly there it was, streaming down the front of his beautiful white jacket. Horrified, she stared at the dark stain spreading all over the white cloth, her mind stunned with shock. 'Oh, your jacket!' she gasped. 'I didn't mean to do that.'

'Didn't you?' His voice was laced with contempt, as

was his glance on her aghast face, as though he was considering her crime more than the expense of replacing the jacket. 'We may as well ruin your dress, too, then we can commiserate with each other.'

Relentlessly he pulled her into his arms, seeking her mouth, his lips bruising against hers, sending her senses reeling. Deliberately, as an agonising flame swept through her, he brought her closer, moulding her sensuously to the hard length of his body. It was a punishment and pain, an angry passion, and Alex felt her blood racing feverishly as she tried to get away. The room whirled as she gulped and gasped, like some poor drowning thing. The scent of sherry was heavy on the air, damp on Chase's skin as he went on holding her and kissing her savagely, taking no notice whatsoever of the twisting, convulsive movements of her protesting limbs.

Her lips were stinging, her whole being enraged that he was kissing her with such intimacy. Blindly her clenched fists beat a helpless tattoo on his shoulders.

Roughly, as he imprisoned her threshing hands, he spoke against her mouth. 'You got a kick out of your big moment, now let me enjoy mine.'

'No!' With surprising determination, she pushed back, catching him unawares. Instead of tightening, his arms slackened and suddenly she was free. Involuntarily, her hand lifted to slap him sharply on the cheek. Might as well be damned completely, she thought wildly, as she saw his fury.

As he muttered a smothered oath, she fled, stumbling across the polished floor up the stairs to her room. The splendid length of the wide staircase had never seemed so endless, and she couldn't tell if it was her heart or his footsteps pounding in her ears. The lights flickered, dancing as she tried to put more distance between them, while her mind tried to convince her there was no need to panic. Chase Marshall was a man of the world. This alone would never allow him to pursue a girl recklessly, frightening her nearly to death!

Or would he? While she had ruined his jacket and shirt, expense-wise this would mean nothing to him. It was the way she had done it—or the way he thought she had done it—which had aroused his anger. Slapping his face hadn't helped either! Normally, he might have shrugged such an incident off as of little consequence, but somehow she had managed to get under his skin. This, she suspected, maddened him as much as her refusal to marry him. Why wouldn't he take her word that she didn't want to marry anyone?

Breathlessly she reached the safety of her bedroom, but to her alarm he was right behind her, slamming the door. Before coming after her he had thrown off his jacket, but there was still the wine-soaked front of his shirt. Tearing open the buttons down the front, he rapped, 'You can apologise, and properly! And if you don't care for the sight of a half naked man in your room, you'd better make it quick. I don't intend steeping in sherry all night.'

'Get out!' Her eyes blazed in her small face. 'Why should I apologise?'

His eyes blazed back, their effect much greater. 'You didn't think you'd get off without making one, did you?'

Apprehensively, Alex gulped. Chase Marshall was a gentleman—master of Coolabra and heaven knows how much more. She hadn't thought ever to see him as angry as this! 'You're making a great drama out of nothing,' she gasped.

He answered between his teeth. 'You deliberately provoke me when God knows I have enough to do. No girl in her right senses would turn down what I've offered.'

'It must comfort you to think so.'

'Shut up!' he grated. 'Be quiet or . . .' He didn't wait

to utter his threat. Like a man driven, he brought her violently to him, his mouth hitting hers with such force it knocked the breath from her body. His grip on her was iron-hard, as though he was determined this time she wouldn't escape him.

Alex was gasping for breath before he lifted his head. Weakened and trembling from his ravaging fury, she lay helpless in his arms. It was too much for her, she couldn't continue fighting him. Her mind rebelled, yet she was stunned by the force of her own awakening desire. What was it about this man that he could arouse emotions she hadn't known existed?

His fingers bruised her soft skin as he tilted up her chin. 'I want an end to this nonsense,' he said curtly, his eyes glittering. 'Both my time and my patience are coming to an end.'

'You can't make me feel guilty,' she whispered, shaking uncontrollably. 'You're the one who should be feeling guilty—being in my room. A woman's room!'

'It's a long time since my conscience bothered me about anything like that,' he drawled sarcastically.

'I don't doubt it!' she all but spat, temper and another, more indefinable emotion making her eyes glow. 'But not here, I think, I suspect you don't usually insult your sister's guests at Coolabra.'

'So my lovemaking is an insult, is it? At last we're getting to the truth!' His hand, curling around her slender neck, slipped inside her thin bodice. 'Come on,' he taunted, 'I may as well hear the lot. What more have you festering in that narrow little mind of yours?'

'Nothing flattering, I assure you!'

Cold anger was in his voice as he snapped, 'Let me tell you how far your refusal to see reason has been responsible for your own downfall. When I first saw you I didn't take you seriously, but I do now.'

Alex was too muddled to work that out. She stared at him, frantically trying to understand, despairing that she was unable to. 'You're making too much out of this, Chase. You've let an idea build up until it's got out of proportion. If only you'd stop and think!'

'Are you implying that I don't know my own mind?' His fingers lay still against the unsteady pulse in her throat as his eyes went slowly and insolently over her. 'When I first saw you I wanted you, and it's a feeling that's been growing ever since.'

She went limp, exhausted from fighting someone so much stronger than herself. Maybe if she kept quiet? Yet how could she, when the glitter in Chase's eyes spoke so clearly of danger? 'You have to get out of here,' she pleaded unsteadily.

'Not yet. You can put up with me a little longer,' he growled, moving her zip with such swift expertise that she gasped. Her dress hit the floor in a silken heap before she had time to realise what was happening.

'Chase!' Her voice cracked as she jerked away from him. 'You're mad!'

'If I'm going mad why not join me?' he jeered, hauling her back to him, his mouth coming down on hers again as he lifted her.

The mattress gave beneath their combined weight and she was crushed. Under his sensual attack her senses ran riot, consuming her mind in hot swirling waves. He kissed her face, her eyes, her throat as he slowly but surely removed the rest of her clothing. In vain her slender body shuddered and jerked as Chase flung off his shirt and dragged her close, his mouth parting hers with a shattering urgency.

The harsh pressure of his lips aroused a frightening storm of feeling. It swept through her, devastating as a flood, with as little mercy, the force of it shutting out the rest of the world, isolating them completely. Unconsciously she edged closer as his hands sought the taut fullness of her breasts, her fingers creeping to his neck and gripping tightly as his hands went lower. Then there was only a wild rush of sensation, promising ecstasy.

'Alex!' he muttered hoarsely. 'I want you—you torment me. You want me, too.'

'Want. . .?' she groaned, his words filling her ears but making little sense. Perhaps he was right. They must want each other, for surely such an all-consuming whirlwind of passion didn't lie. It wrenched their bodies with a feverish impatience to be one. Which might have brought the peace of utter fulfilment, if they had been in love. That Chase didn't love her stood out in the inflamed recess of her mind like a red light. This way, it flashed a stark message, lay danger.

She felt his strong thighs against hers, pressing restively, making her instinctively aware, from his gasping groan, that his control was going. His breathing quickened, his mouth crushing hers with renewed urgency as his hand went to his belt, ripping it off.

She felt weak but vibrantly excited. She couldn't fight him, he was altogether too much for her, nor was she sure now that she wanted to. His weight pinned her down, she was helpless as it forced her surrender. Desperately she clutched at his broad shoulders as he bent over her. She felt as though she was drowning yet was quite willing to sink beneath the waves. They were hitting her now, great waves of mutual desire, dragging her breathlessly under.

Then suddenly she was free. The blood still roared in her ears, but she could hear the harsh, agonised rasp of his breathing as Chase let her go.

'Cover yourself up!' He rolled away from her, burying his face against a pillow, his hands clenched above his head, his whole body taut.

After a few brief moments, while Alex tried numbly to do as she was told, he rose to his feet, refastened his belt and reached for his shirt. 'Be thankful I want to give Coolabra an unsullied bride,' he said coldly.

'Which I will do, unless you continue to be stubborn.'

The contempt in his voice, so clearly conveying a belief that he could have had her there and then, had he so desired, turned her shame to rage. 'I won't ever be your bride!' she cried recklessly, clutching the sheet so tightly around her it might have torn. 'For one thing, I could never hope to live up to you. My ignorance could never match such expertise!'

Sitting down on the edge of the bed, Chase began buttoning his shirt with steady fingers, the derision in his eyes cutting through her. 'We all have to start somewhere,' he mocked. 'and if that's all you're worrying about, I should advise you to forget it. At the rate you were going you'd soon be ahead of me. Once I had you, I fancy you'd soon be back for more.'

'Please get out of my bedroom!' she choked, her cheeks scarlet. When he made no move to do as she asked immediately, she hissed, 'Why are you treating me like a—a slut, and talking to me like this? Your aunt would be horrified. I can hardly believe it myself. You're acting like a—a . . .'

'A normal man?' he suggested silkily. 'We're all much the same underneath, you know, Alex Latham. We may go around in different guises, but underneath, when it comes down to basics, there's not much difference. But don't forget I do want to marry you,' his mouth twisted sardonically. 'Remember that when you're getting all uptight and insulted. If I'd wanted an illicit relationship I certainly wouldn't have stopped when I did.'

CHAPTER SEVEN

WORDLESSLY, Alex watched Chase leave her. His dark gaze rested on her angry face before he rose to his feet again and walked out of her room. Alex would liked to have thrown something, she felt so infuriated by his hidebound arrogance. He seemed to imagine he had merely to lift a finger to get anything he wanted! He said all men were the same, yet how many would get away with half the things he did? Arrogance and authority sat on his broad shoulders so naturally, people automatically accepted it, but wasn't it time he met with a little opposition? She had refused to marry him and would keep on refusing. It might do him no harm to learn what it felt like to cry for the moon!

Weakly, when most of her anger spent itself, she lay back on her pillows. How would she feel if Chase walked out of her life—eventually defeated? Something clutched at her heart, tearing painfully through it. He was right about one thing. When she was in his arms she forgot about everything else. Everything else faded. There was only the insistent pressure of his arms and lips, the intense, excited reactions of her own body, but while she couldn't deny her own eager response, she would never admit this was love.

Yet how could she tell? Wearily she pushed the heavy fair hair from off her hot brow. It wasn't a question she wanted to pursue, for Chase certainly didn't love her. This alone would make marriage impossible, even if she had been tempted—which she wasn't! Apart from a natural aversion to being pushed into marriage, it would never work, not for her with Chase Marshall. He was too strong, too ruggedly dominating. At the height of passion—to which she bitterly had little doubt he could raise her—she might easily moan out her love for him and have her burning ears filled with his mocking derisive laughter. Not that she was ever likely to be in love with him, she hastened to assure herself, as she slipped quickly into an exhausted, restless sleep.

As the wedding day drew nearer, and Alex grew even busier, she thought it would become easier to keep Chase at the back of her mind. This, however, proved far from easy as, at every turn, he appeared to be there. At first she thought it must simply be coincidental until she realised that for him such a word didn't exist. Things happened the way he planned, not because of some untidy act of fate.

Down at the pool he joined Ruby and her for coffee. He made a point, now, of always appearing for lunch. Here his attention to Alex was limited to keeping her wine glass topped up and passing a frequent but casual remark. His eyes, though, often lingered on her remarkable young beauty and once he had called her darling, in front of the others. Admittedly, it was during an argument, and he had used a lightly mocking tone, but it had been enough to bring an enchanting rose colour to her smooth cheeks. She felt Ruby glance at them quickly, and Miss Harriet's surprised stare, but Chase's expression was bland, even slightly amused behind a glitter that was cruel. Alex's pulse began racing as he held her a prisoner with his eyes. For all she tried she had been unable to look away. It wasn't until Miss Harriet hastily asked his opinion about a minor problem in the kitchen that he released her.

Apart from this, he didn't actually step up the pace noticeably until the wedding day. It was then that he stayed by her side so continually it began to attract attention. Frequently, now, he called her darling, and apparently didn't care who heard. He did it, she suspected deliberately, and she hated it. When, exasperated beyond measure, she protested fiercely, he merely raised taunting eyebrows.

'Aren't you pleased to be stealing some of the bride's limelight?'

'Actually no.' She gripped the edge of the table she was standing beside for support. 'What you're doing could set up a whole chain of unnecessary gossip.'

'But nothing that mightn't be true?' His eyes glinting, he stared down at the lovely picture she made in her wedding day finery. A new dress which she had been forced to ask her mother to send, and in which, had she but known it, she looked tantalisingly adorable. His glance slid from the high, tilted breasts to the narrow little waist and back again, pausing to examine the accelerating pulse in her throat. 'In that dress you're enough to make any man lose his sense of discretion.'

'I hate you!' she raged, unable to think of anything more telling.

'Then you'd better be prepared to hate me more,' he grinned, grasping her arm, carrying her along with him as, the ceremony over, they followed the bride and groom to the reception.

Ruby made a beautiful bride; it was generally agreed that her wedding dress must have cost a small fortune. It was heavily embroidered white satin that suited Ruby's sophisticated darkness extremely well. Henry looked happy and handsome, a wry smile on his face as he rather clumsily held Ruby's train out of the way so she could sit down.

Tentatively, Alex glanced from him to Chase, aware that he couldn't compare with Chase for bearing and looks. In his morning coat, Chase was superbly handsome, drawing a great deal of feminine attention from the bride and groom. That he also drew many speculative eyes to Alex, by being constantly at her side, was something she wholly resented. Especially as he was obviously not prepared to remedy the situation by leaving her.

A famous firm of caterers had been called in, so everything in that direction was well taken care of. The tables were beautifully set, the food and wine of the very finest quality. Everything was exactly as it should be for a Marshall wedding. No one would go away able to find fault with one thing. If there was such a possibility, Alex thought wryly, stealing a glance at Chase under her long lashes, she had no doubt someone's head would roll! Chase Marshall would pay the best and expect it, heaven help anyone who let him down! Sighing, she looked away from him, across the wide marquee.

'Your turn next, my dear.' A middle-aged matron, too obviously searching for something more sensational than a bride and bridegroom, managed to catch Alex's eye gushingly.

Chase's attentive glance and his firm, 'I don't doubt it,' brought a quite audible gasp from the lady as well as interested glances from those around.

Alex, incensed, was about to get up and walk out when she felt his fingers fasten on her arm. In a low voice he told her curtly to stay where she was. 'If you run away I'll bring you back,' he threatened, 'if I have to carry you!'

He made her sit by him throughout the reception, which was long and split by numerous speeches and toasts. Alex had never felt so disturbed in her life, especially as it was easy to see both Ruby and Miss Harriet were clearly curious as to why she was seated where she was. Chase must be the only one enjoying this, she decided mutinously. Even when he was on his feet, making what turned out to be the best speech of the day, she was conscious of him looking down on her too frequently.

'You're doing it deliberately!' she accused, shaking with nerves as he acknowledged the loud applause and sat down. 'I don't know what you intend . . .'

'To marry you,' he cut in coldly, his hard mouth set, as he stared into her vivid blue eyes. 'One way or another, as I've already told you. And if you don't marry me after this week I think you'll soon be feeling very sorry for yourself. Everyone loves a budding romance, my dear, but they appreciate a girl who's been rejected more.'

'In this case, I'm rejecting you.'

'Ah, but who would believe it?' His smile was harsh, suddenly far from lover-like. 'If some of the ladies here ever get their claws into you, my darling, your reputation will be in shreds. Then what will Mummy say?'

'You're a fiend!'

'Then I shouldn't make a dull husband.'

'I don't want one of any kind.'

'I think you do.' His hand on her arm gentled, his fingers moving sensuously over the soft skin. 'You'd better wake up to yourself, Alex Latham, before it's too late. Quite seriously I'm telling you, you're highly inflammable material. One of these days you could go up in a blue light, with a man who isn't your husband.' His grip slid to her wrist, again unobtrusively measuring the pulse rate, as colour came wildly to her face. 'I've had you in my arms, remember? I should know.'

He was outrageous, a swine! For once she didn't care if her thoughts weren't particularly ladylike. Sometimes she got tired to death of being a lady. Chase Marshall was forever provoking her. He enjoyed having her either deathly pale or blushing like a rose. Shivering, she tore her tortured eyes away from his. Now he was trying to shock her. Didn't he realise she would have to love a man before she gave herself completely?

Shortly after the reception was over, Ruby and Henry left on a European honeymoon. A lot of guests went to the airstrip to see them off and afterwards there was dancing and other entertainment, which went on all night. Chase, as host, was duty bound to dance with the other women guests, but he danced with Alex most. She was still on her feet at two in the morning, surprised at her own vitality and looking as pretty and delicate as a flower in her lovely chiffon dress floating around her, her soft fair hair falling in a silky cloud about her shoulders.

She had spent a lot of time with a young man of about twenty-five, who owned a cattle station near Darwin. Rex Clyde was nice, a perfect gentleman, she thought, and good fun. He pursued Alex quite blatantly, but she found she enjoyed his company and had no compunction about dancing with him frequently. On one occasion she and Rex had the floor to themselves, as he guided her into a kind of complicated Spanish tango. Alex, though no expert, was supple and light on her feet and managed to give quite a good account of herself. It certainly earned a goodnatured round of applause when she laughingly gave up a few minutes later.

Rex was complimenting her on her performance when Chase broke in. 'You don't mind, Rex, if I have my partner back?' He sounded as if it was costing him an effort to be polite. Without waiting for a reply he swept her away. It was a dreamy waltz, but she felt anything but dreamy.

'There was no need to say that, Chase. You have no special claim on me.'

His grip tightened as she tried to draw away from him. 'You know all about the claim I have on you.' His voice was like steel. 'You're going to marry me, your acceptance just being a matter of time, and I won't have my future wife making an exhibition of herself on a dance floor. Clyde should know better. I'll certainly have a word with him about it.'

'You're welcome to try, but I'm sure he won't listen,' she retorted, wondering, as her voice rose, why being in Chase Marshall's arms could stir her so deeply, when in Rex's arms she hadn't felt a thing.

'Keep your voice down!' Chase said curtly, 'unless

you want everyone staring at you again.' His face darkened as he gazed down on her. 'Remember where you are.'

'I'm not likely to be given a chance to forget, am I?' she replied furiously. 'I expect I should feel honoured just to be here, not to mention being chosen for your special attention.'

'Alex, will you be quiet! I don't want to make you, but I won't be provoked.' When she would have stopped dancing, his thigh pressed hard against hers, forcing her to continue, his hand tightening on her waist, causing her stomach to turn over.

On a little gasp she protested, 'Chase, I wish you wouldn't! You're hurting me!'

His lips clamped, a look of taut anger hardening his face. 'How did you guess?' he asked suavely. Then, 'Aren't you tired yet?'

Thinking he was going to suggest she went to bed, she smiled contrarily. 'No, not a bit.'

'Good,' he rejoined mockingly. 'If you're not tired then a walk in the garden won't be too much for you. We can continue this argument outside.'

They had left the crowded marquee and were out among the trees, almost before Alex knew what was happening. Chase's hold on her arm didn't relax until they had gone some distance—distance she scarcely recalled covering.

The garden was dark and this particular corner of it secluded. The night air was still warm and heavily scented. To gain a little courage, Alex breathed deeply, only to find the sweet, sensuous scents swaying her senses.

'Let me go!' she cried, suddenly wary as he turned her to him. 'If I shout for help someone will hear me!'

'Rex, perhaps?' As if what she said infuriated him, he added curtly, 'We must make sure he doesn't.'

'Chase!' she protested, as he lowered his head, silencing her voice beneath the force of his mouth.

There was no point in her struggling, she thought wildly, as his arms went round her like bands of steel. He was strong enough to crush any resistance. As always, when he kissed her, she could only think of one kind of defence—that if she didn't struggle he might lose interest. Why couldn't she learn it was always otherwise? The flame that immediately joined them together was growing too powerful to be so easily disposed of.

Not wishing to give him the satisfaction of knowing how much his kisses affected her, she twisted frantically against him, unwittingly arousing him more than she might otherwise have done. He threaded harsh fingers through her hair, shaping the back of her head, holding her remorselessly until she quietened and lay fully acquiescent, trembling from the sensuous exploration of his mouth.

Her heart racing, she sensed his satisfaction at her helpless response to his lovemaking. From the beginning he had dominated, invading first her mind and then her senses. She might have forgiven him if he hadn't fought such a deliberate campaign, if he had once kissed her because he couldn't help himself. She might have forgiven herself for responding so feverishly in his arms if her passion had concealed even one feasible plan of escape.

As he felt her struggles weaken, his inexorable grip slackened to allow her arms to creep blindly around his neck. His mouth wandered as he muttered words thickly, releasing a stream of feeling from every nerve centre he touched. Now she didn't even bother trying to soothe her muddled conscience—she felt separated from it, lost in his strength. Urgently her fingers tightened on his dark head, bringing his hungry mouth back to hers, and he claimed her mouth with such deep intensity she could only quiver.

For the moment he wasn't attempting to check himself. His strong, well shaped hands held her to him, lingering on each warm curve of her body. caressing until she was wholly yielding, her skin overheated, her slim arms as urgent as his. She didn't know what he was trying to prove, but he was stirring her to the point of exhausted tears. The other night he had succeeded in arousing her dormant sensuality, but she thought she had it under control. Now he had her trembling, stirred to the point where she only longed for release or oblivion, uncaring about anything else any more.

Chase put her from him abruptly, able to withdraw with an ease she bitterly envied. He had recovered his usual authoritative hardness, but there was a slight, triumphant smile on his lips. 'Alex, much as I'd like to carry you to my bed, I'll have to restrain myself.' As she swayed, he asked sharply, 'Are you all right?' Then, as she nodded dumbly, he added, 'I don't mind giving our guests something to talk about, providing it's the right kind of thing. Might I announce our engagement tomorrow?'

'No!' Alex had conditioned herself so thoroughly to this answer, she had no hestiation. 'You have no right . . .'

'One day soon, you have to give in to me.' Anger smouldered in his eyes at her continual resistance. Pride demanded she gave in to him. She could see it in his face and it repelled her, even as her excited heart whispered that it might be the most wonderful thing she could do.

'No,' she repeated steadily.

His laughter was harsh as he turned her back towards the marquee. He took little notice of her pale face and dragging steps. 'If you don't give in,' he threatened, 'I must find a way of making you. One day soon you might find yourself left with no other choice but to say yes.'

'You've said that before,' she muttered unhappily.

'No harm in saying it again,' he returned savagely.

Shortly after this the party broke up, though it was doubtful if many went to bed. The house was full as many people were staying over. Bedrooms and every spare corner seemed packed with people trying to snatch an hour's sleep. Others just gave up and had breakfast, after which they appeared fully able to face another day. Alex was amazed at the ability many displayed to keep going almost indefinitely!

Time and again she was surprised at her own energy, but by the end of the week she was beginning to wonder how much she had left. She felt curiously exhausted, not even inclined to argue when, after the last guests had gone, Chase insisted firmly that she spent the next few days quietly.

They were having coffee in the lounge after lunch with Aunt Harriet, just the three of them, and when Chase spoke Alex found herself smiling at him gratefully, thinking she might be well advised to do just that.

Aunt Harriet regarded her affectionately. 'You've done remarkably well, dear. You've been a great help. I'm sure Ruby's wedding wouldn't have gone off half as well without you.'

Alex shivered, thinking she must have picked up more from her mother than she realised. Mrs Latham could organise anything—she had it down to a fine art, but Alex hoped she would never trample over people the way her mother often did.

Chase teased blandly, 'By the time Alex has been here a few years she'll have quite a reputation. In less than that, I would say, if she agrees to stay.'

Again Aunt Harriet beamed. 'I do hope you will, Alex. I'm only just beginning to realise how wonderful it is to have a kind of general assistant. Mrs Young is good, but I can't expect her to do things like writing my letters and coping with visitors. She has more than enough to do as it is.'

'Well, I'm afraid I can't stay much longer,' Alex began, feeling trapped again. In the face of Miss Harriet's eagerness it was difficult to say she must leave immediately, which of course she must! She hadn't seen nearly enough of Coolabra, she doubted if she ever would, but it was growing more imperative each day that she got away from Chase. Twice since Ruby's wedding, he had asked her to marry him. Both times she had refused. The last time she had flinched from his cold anger, anger which she fancied for once had nearly got out of control. With the effort of pulling himself together, he appeared to come to a decision—exactly what, Alex couldn't guess, but it still made her shiver to recall his expression. Each day she became more aware of a danger which seemed only to grow.

'You must stay here until I get back,' Chase surprised her by saying. Aunt Harriet, apparently not taking Alex's protests at all seriously, hurried off to consult with Mrs Young.

'Until you come back?' Alex faltered stupidly, wondering why he was watching her like a cat watches a mouse. 'I—I didn't know you were going anywhere.'

He smiled tightly, coming to stand close by her as she rose anxiously. 'Didn't anyone tell you? I'm going to Sydney, but I hope to be back by Thursday.'

Alex stared at him, her heart beginning to hammer. 'I could go with you to Brisbane and get a plane back to Melbourne.'

'No,' he made a soft jeering noise in his throat, 'nothing doing. You'll be here to welcome me when I return—and if you're a good girl, I might bring you a surprise.'

Her blue eyes widened with a growing despair. Hadn't she been right to suspect he was planning something? 'I don't want a surprise,' she said fiercely, 'I just want to leave. When are you going?'

'Drew's waiting to run me out to the airstrip.'

'Now?' It was a shattering shock. Her eyes went quickly to his dark pants and shirt, the kind of clothes he wore when he wasn't out on the station with the men, ideally suited for travelling to any major city. No, just by looking at his clothes she couldn't have guessed. And in Sydney he would have his flat and plenty of business suits.

'Yes, I'm going now,' he assured her coolly, mocking her obvious if silent attempts to think of a way she might foil him. 'You can come to the strip and see me off, but that's as far as you're going.'

Refusing to give up, Alex followed him out, only too willing to grab the chance of a few extra minutes in which there might still be some faint possibility of him changing his mind. 'Why didn't you tell me sooner?' she asked.

'Because, my darling, you would only have pestered me worse than you're doing now, and this in the first peaceful day we've had in weeks.'

Drew had his bag stowed away in the back of the truck, but it was to the front of it that Chase steered Alex. Quickly he swung her up between Drew and himself, then they were off. She dared not protest, not even when he put his arm around her, supposedly to steady her when the truck lurched over rough patches. From her waist his hand slipped to her thigh and she was aware of his slight, taunting smile as she wriggled.

At the airstrip the plane waited, but Alex knew it was hopeless. Seldom, outside fiction, did girls manage to stow away. She didn't stand a chance.

Chase, watching her narrowly, read her thoughts and shook his head. 'Not a chance,' he confirmed, shaking his head. He put his arms around her shoulders again, drawing her closer, his eyes darkening as he stared into her resentful ones. 'Kiss me goodbye,' he demanded thickly.

As his head bent she was aware of Drew Blake turn-

ing tactfully away, and her resentment grew that Chase
was embarrassing her deliberately. Unless she was prepared to make a scene she must give him the kiss he
sought. To get it over quickly she lifted her lips in apparent obedience.

His claim on her mouth was absolute. Swiftly he
brushed aside her endeavours to keep it light and brief.
His arms tightened cruelly around her slight body as he
forced her mouth open under his.

Attempting to stiffen, she was immediately betrayed
by her own abandoned response. Her arms went around
his neck and she clung to him, her mouth clinging, too,
moving softly under his in a kind of helpless passion.

When Chase released her he stared down at her face
for a few motionless seconds, his eyes smouldering with
undisguised desire. 'Yet you still keep on saying no!'
Abruptly he left her, speaking to Drew, the words he
had spoken to her still ringing derisively in her ears.

During the next few days she found it difficult to
settle to anything, although she told herself she should
be glad of the respite his absence gave. Aunt Harriet
had apparently known of Chase's trip, but declared she
hadn't thought to mention it. Alex, considering this
darkly, wasn't sure whether to believe or not. Sometimes she was sure there was a huge conspiracy against
her. When asked if she missed Chase, Aunt Harriet
admitted she did, but that she was used to his being
away. She seemed reluctant to discuss it, but assured
Alex he always came back.

It did occur to Alex that there might be nothing to prevent her escaping from Coolabra while Chase was gone.
She didn't know what orders he had left, but she was
certain he wouldn't have stated specifically that she
wasn't to leave the station. Instinct, however, warned
her to be cautious, so she made her first enquiries discreetly.

Again she approached Aunt Harriet. 'I'd like to do

some shopping in Mount Isa. Do you think you could spare me?' Her conscience bothered her over deceiving Aunt Harriet about this, but it seemed the only way.

Aunt Harriet glanced at her sharply. 'I might,' she replied carefully, 'but I don't think anyone could be spared to take you. Drew's very busy with the mustering, I believe.'

Anxiously, Alex protested. 'I don't really mind about Drew. Perhaps one of the other men could go?'

Aunt Harriet shook her head. 'Maybe later in the week,' she said vaguely. 'Of course you can always go and ask Drew.'

'If you gave him a definite order?' Alex suggested desperately.

'Oh, but I couldn't do that, dear child,' Aunt Harriet declared, quite unconvincingly.

Determined not to give up easily, Alex went immediately to see Chase's manager. 'Couldn't you find time to take me?' she begged.

'I'm afraid not.' No more helpful than Aunt Harriet, Drew smiled evasively, 'Not for a few days, anyway.'

When Chase would be back again! Contrary to what she had thought, it was becoming abundantly clear he had left orders—of some sort! Trying to hide her rising anger behind a charming smile, she persevered. 'You can't tell me that you haven't one man available. Why, since I've been here I've seen dozens.'

'And every one with a job to do, I'm afraid.' He grinned warmly down at her lovely little face, almost beginning to believe in angels. 'Why not let me take you out riding? On the boss's orders, mind you. Chase suggested it himself.'

'No, thank you,' she declined sharply, her smile fading as she left him. 'That might take almost as long as a trip to Mount Isa, Drew.'

With all means of escape being unmistakably cut off, Alex found herself thinking of Chase constantly. It dawned on her suddenly, one day in the garden, that she didn't want to run from him any more. Suddenly she was stunned by the realisation that she cared for him deeply. The knowledge of this love, catching her so unawares, shook her so much she was forced to sit down weakly. She couldn't tell when it had happened, perhaps it had been there all the time, fighting to make itself known behind the hate she had been convinced was all she felt for him. She might have known, when his kisses set her on fire, that the rapture she experienced in his arms could never be founded on hate. Her whole body warmed to the memory of his lovemaking and she longed to be in his arms again.

Blindly she stumbled to her feet, wandering the entire length of the garden, reaching a wilder part of it some distance from the house, where she surprised a multitude of brilliantly coloured parakeets. Today, with her thoughts centred completely on Chase, she scarcely noticed their wild beauty. That she loved him didn't change anything. Chase had kissed her hungrily on the airstrip, but he had no love for her. Like her mother, he was entirely dominating, determined always to have his own way. To marry him would simply be exchanging one form of bondage for another, and a husband would be much more difficult to escape than a mother!

It was only as the hours and days passed, ever more slowly, that Alex began to change her mind. She was missing Chase desperately. The nights were so long she sometimes passed them in crying, burying her hot cheeks in the pillows, unable to rest. The emptiness of being without him used up all her nervous strength so that her days were spoilt by frequent headaches and anxious shadows darkened her eyes. If she was to capitulate and marry Chase, surely nothing could be worse than what she was suffering now. And it would be her own decision. Chase wouldn't be a husband chosen by her mother. Her mother hadn't had anything to do with it. If she wasn't strong enough to go on refusing to marry him, this one factor would make it easier to accept.

Nothing was heard from Chase until he had been away four days—days when time seemed to be standing still, for all Alex managed to pack into them. It made her conscious of how lonely she was on her own, something she had never been aware of before. She loved the station—the isolation didn't daunt her, and she could find so much to keep herself occupied, but without Chase it was as if the axle on which she rotated had been removed. When he sent word by Drew Blake that he was coming home, the surge of joy she felt shook her.

'He's been gone a long time,' she exclaimed, her small face so radiant that Drew and Aunt Harriet glanced quickly at each other before looking away.

'Well,' said Aunt Harriet, with a slight smile, 'it will be nice to have him back. Was there any other message, Drew?'

'No—er——' somehow Drew found it necessary to stare at the floor, 'that was about all.'

Alex, murmuring an excuse, left them, feeling suddenly a great desire to be alone. Finding her favourite spot in the garden, she lingered there for some time before returning to the house. Going up to her room to rinse her face and hands before tea, she bumped into Mrs Young coming down, looking flustered.

It was so seldom that Mrs Young was put out over anything that, startled, Alex paused. 'Is there something wrong, Mrs Young? Can I help?'

'No, dear, it's all taken care of. Chase is bringing a lady guest and I've had a room to prepare in a hurry. Normally, it should have been ready, but we still seem to be at sixes and sevens from the wedding.'

A lady-friend? Alex went on her way, her heart like a

stone in her breast. So that was why Drew had looked confused earlier? It would be Davina, of course. Or it could be someone else. Chase, she thought bitterly, might have no compunction about casting off the old to get on with the new.

Yet could she blame him? Sickly she decided she could not. Hadn't she refused to marry him often enough? Once too often, it would seem. This was why he had insisted she stayed until he returned—so he could take his revenge. He had known Alex was attracted to him. He had wanted marriage for the sake of Coolabra and been annoyed by her continual refusals. Now he was bringing with him a girl who must be only too eager to be his wife. He might even intend asking Alex to help with the arranging of another wedding!

Tears began running unhappily down Alex's cheeks, and she had cried too much lately. Quickly she scrubbed them away with her knuckles. She must pull herself together. No one must be allowed to guess she was feeling miserable, least of all Chase. It might take effort, but it couldn't be for long. With any luck she could be back in Melbourne tomorrow. He would have to let her go after this. Under no circumstances would she consider staying on. Her heart might be breaking, but she must prove she still had some pride.

She waited until she heard the faint sound of an engine. Catching a painful breath, she listened to it approaching, the noise of the truck growing louder until it stopped outside. Drew had brought Chase and his lady-friend from the airstrip. The sudden silence, then the murmur of voices, brought this information winging to Alex's room.

Taking herself firmly in hand, she rejected a distracted inclination to stay upstairs until it was time for dinner. By then she might only feel worse and there were things she must have settled by then. Her own departure being one of them.

Smoothing her silky sundress over the slender curve of her hips, she reached for the zip and drew it up carefully. The soft material shaped the lovely curve of her breasts, the neckline cut just low enough to allow a tantalising glimpse of them. It was the kind of dress which she normally kept for a smart sunbathing party, rather than for afternoon tea, but today she felt greatly in need of something to give her a little extra confidence.

Quickly she ran a comb through her hair, relieved that it was looking particularly beautiful. This afternoon, she realised, glancing in her mirror, it was the best thing about her—that and her figure. Yesterday her face had glowed, because of her incredibly misguided decision to marry Chase. Now it was lifeless, distraught and pale. Despairingly she pinched her cheeks, hoping to induce a little colour.

Downstairs she heard voices again, this time coming from the lounge, the one which opened on to the front of the house. For a moment Alex paused, staring at the closed door. Chase had promised her a surprise and at least she was partly prepared for it. Taking a deep breath, she opened the door, a smile fixed stiffly on her white face.

As the door swung soundlessly open and she stepped over the threshold, she stopped sharply, clutching the door handle with icy fingers, feeling she was about to faint. Seated by Aunt Harriet, looking completely at ease, was her mother.

CHAPTER EIGHT

HER eyes wide with an apprehension she didn't yet fully understand, Alex stood staring at her mother. Vaguely she was aware of Chase coming between them, and that her mother hadn't yet seen her.

Chase had. He strode towards her smiling. 'I was just on my way to see what was keeping you,' he told her, holding out a hand.

Ignoring it, she didn't return his smile. She felt far too stunned to return a gesture of any kind, and in this case she did not want to. 'What's my mother doing here?'

He stopped very near, as if wishing to keep this between the two of them. His eyes went over her swiftly, a flare of anger in their depths at her tone. The smile faded from his deeply moulded mouth, his dark face went hard and tense, a vertical line between his black brows.

As Alex instinctively drew back, his eyes glittered, his brief explanation tinged with a mockery which might not otherwise have been there. 'She came at my invitation,' he drawled. 'Your father is to join us next week. Neither of your parents have actually stayed on a cattle station before. Your father, particularly, is extremely interested.'

Because of his work he would be, but this was beside the point! 'Chase?' Her face was even paler than it had been a few moments ago. 'You don't ask strangers here just because they haven't been Outback before. You had another reason!'

'You might be all the reason I need. Haven't you thought of that?'

Alex felt cornered. She didn't understand it, but she

felt terrible. She put a hand helplessly to her throbbing head. 'You brought my mother here so she could bully me into marrying you!'

'For God's sake, Alex!' he exclaimed harshly, his face almost as pale as her own, 'I don't know what you take me for, but we can't argue about it here.'

Her mother turned, her smile charming as she caught sight of her young daughter. 'Alex darling!' she held out her hands. 'Come and kiss me. Aren't you surprised to see me? I told Mr Marshall you would be, but he said he'd promised you a surprise.'

'So he did. How are you, Mother?' Slowly, her face oddly set, Alex went over to suffer her mother's fond embrace. Her mother, always theatrical, enjoyed such public demonstrations of affection.

'I've never felt better, darling.' After bestowing a cool peck on Alex's cheek, Enid Latham patted an imaginary hair back in place. At fifty, she looked ten years younger and believed in looking after herself. Always beautifully dressed—with her own money, as she was fond of telling her long-suffering husband—she was impeccably groomed. Even Aunt Harriet seemed impressed. Alex was to learn that yet another of Enid's affluent English relatives had died, leaving her a considerable legacy. No one could accuse her mother of not putting the money to good use, Alex thought dryly. To all outward appearances, Enid Latham was a cultured and still beautiful woman.

'You really are a naughty child,' Enid shook her head at Alex sadly. 'Why didn't you tell me about this wonderful place? All we had was one letter, saying you'd arrived safely. Why, we weren't even sure of the address!'

'I—I didn't think I'd be staying long,' Alex replied evasively.

'Never mind,' Enid smiled again, sparkling, 'Mr Marshall explained everything. He's been so kind—making all the arrangements, bringing me all the way here.' She turned to Aunt Harriet. 'I feel quite overwhelmed!'

How did her mother get away with it? Such sugary poise made Alex feel sick! She wouldn't have believed Aunt Harriet could be so taken in, yet she was looking at Enid with a gratifying approval and anticipation. Anyone might be forgiven for thinking she was looking forward to the next few weeks.

Graciously accepting Enid's praise as Coolabra's right, Aunt Harriet inclined her grey head. 'Most people are overwhelmed when they first visit,' she said. Then, reproachfully, she asked Alex, 'Would you mind pouring us a cup of tea, dear, before it gets quite cold. We waited for you.'

Reluctantly but obediently, Alex sat down on the small sofa by which the tea-tray was placed. When Chase sat down beside her she was startled but didn't look at him. His weight on the soft cushion brought her nearer, and she felt her side tingle although they didn't actually touch. It was as if their bodies were reaching out hungrily, with a kind of telepathic instinct of their own. But it was minds that counted, Alex told herself fiercely, and Chase's and hers were miles apart! There was not a bit of sympathy between them, let alone closeness. If there had been he would never have asked her mother here, to help fight a battle he might have won himself—if he had been prepared to use tenderness instead of authority. What a fool she must have been to imagine she could marry a man who did things like this!

Murmuring an apology to Aunt Harriet for keeping her waiting, she gave the ladies their tea, then passed Chase his. Her hands shook slightly with nerves as his fingers brushed hers, but she still refused to meet his eyes, though she felt them steadily upon her.

After tea, during which her silence appeared to go unnoticed against the general flow of conversation, Aunt Harriet suggested Alex took her mother to her room.

'I expect you would like to rest before dinner, Mrs Latham. I hope you'll be comfortable, but be sure and ask if there's anything you want.'

Alex said, 'Yes, of course,' getting to her feet, still without looking at Chase. That Enid was impressed by the house grew more obvious with each step she took. In her room she turned to Alex, her eyes alight.

'I can scarcely believe it! Oh, do close the door, darling, and sit down for a minute. I never dreamt you would fall on your feet like this!'

Alex's lips moved with difficulty, as she stood where she was. 'Whatever are you talking about, Mother? I'm here to work. As soon as possible I'll be returning to Melbourne. Perhaps within the next few days.'

Smiling lightly, Enid pretended not to hear. 'Mr Marshall, Chase, is charming. A really splendid man. When he came to the house and introduced himself both your father and I were impressed. We both agreed we'd never met anyone like him, and your father says he must be a millionaire several times over!'

'How nice for him.'

'Yes, isn't it?' Suddenly Enid frowned, conscious of her daughter's lack of enthusiasm. 'I shouldn't pass any more remarks like that, if I were you. Although you pretend to despise it, money does talk.'

'I'll take your word for it,' Alex returned, unnaturally flippant.

'Alex!'

'What about Don Fisher?' she asked wildly, feeling she would rather attack than be attacked. She recognised her mother's tactics a mile off.

'Don Fisher? Oh,' he might have been a man Enid had scarcely heard of, 'I believe someone said he's gone off somewhere. I haven't seen him for a while.'

'And your English friend?'

'Monica's gone to visit some cousins in Perth, but it's Chase I want to talk about, darling.'

'Some other time, Mother. I have things to do. You'll

have to excuse me.' Seething with disgust, Alex almost ran from the room. She would liked to have gone for a long walk or ride, but was frightened of bumping into Chase. Before meeting him again she must be in a calmer frame of mind. A girl had to be very calm indeed to hold her own against Chase Marshall.

Still hurrying, she reached her own room, having decided to have a quick shower and go down early to give Mrs Young a hand. Chase might not approve, but she wasn't too concerned about that.

It seemed to put the crowning touch to a terrible afternoon to find Chase waiting for her in her room. He was stretched out on the bed, as though he had every right to be there, and Alex shuddered to think what her mother would have made of that, had she been here with her!

'Are you mad?' Alex asked, staring at him.

Lazily he swung his long legs to the floor, sitting easily on the edge of the bed and regarding her steadily. 'No, I'm not mad,' he replied coolly, 'but I soon might be if you don't stop acting like a spoiled child. And the madness I'm talking of is anger, not insanity.'

'You're welcome to stay,' she hissed, 'for exactly two seconds. Now, what do you want?'

Suddenly there was menace in him, enough to make her hesitate over making too free with her tongue. His brilliant eyes trained on her narrowly, he said, 'We have to talk . . .'

'You seem to have gone more in for action,' she retorted coldly, outwardly very cool, inwardly shaking. 'Why did you bring my mother here? And you can answer quite freely, we aren't downstairs now!'

'Why not?' His dark eyes flickered over her, a hard light in them. 'I do happen to have honourable intentions, something that seems constantly to escape your notice. I thought it was about time I met your family and had them visit mine. Naturally your parents are concerned for you. It was up to me to reassure them about their future son-in-law.'

The colour seeped suddenly from under Alex's skin. 'I haven't agreed to marry you!' Her voice was a mere thread of sound and she knew she looked frightened.

'I've said nothing to make them believe you have.'

Her heart racing, she remembered she had almost decided to tell him she would marry him, when he came back. But for her mother's arrival she might already have been committed. Chase might not know it, but he had ruined everything by bringing her mother to Coolabra. The thing was, she thought bitterly, there was no way she could explain this and make it sound sensible. When she had thought it was Davina he was bringing with him this afternoon, it had been a shock, but not worse than this. Her eyes widened despairingly. 'I don't know what's going on, but I believe you brought my mother here to try and talk some sense into me. I'm not so stupid I can't understand that!'

Chase's strongly curved mouth had a curious white ring around it, but his voice was sardonic. 'I wish you loved me half as much as you love jumping to the wrong conclusions. I think you've got your mother all wrong. Admittedly she's self-assured, but she was born that way—it had nothing to do with you. She can no more help wishing to see you well settled than she can help her own nature. But she's abrasive, rather than cloying. A doer—which is perhaps better than being one of those who just sit and think about getting something done. Once we were married she would soon turn her organising fervour elsewhere. You would be in no further danger.'

'Only married to you.'

'You consider that would be worse?'

Alex couldn't answer, she didn't know what to say. He was shockingly frank, but as if with some purpose. He seemed to be trying to make her understand something, but she was so confused she couldn't think what. He had talked a lot, but she sensed the really important things he had deliberately left unsaid.

He came over to her then, grasping her shoulders, no tenderness either in his hands or eyes. 'You have a lot of sorting out to do yourself, Alex, otherwise you won't ever be able to stick to any decision you make. You will simply believe it was my will, and your mother's, imposed over yours, and that would be no good to either of us.'

Tears stung the back of her eyes. 'What a pleasure it's going to be, having you both standing over me!'

'Oh, come on, child!' his glance was suddenly kinder. 'I'm no monster, though I can see I'm going to have my work cut out convincing you. Let's forget about marriage for the time being.'

'You've said that before, yet you keep on asking.'

'Maybe I'll wait until you ask, next time,' he rejoined grimly.

'That's a relief,' Alex retorted recklessly. 'Now I can forget it.'

His face darkened. 'I won't promise not to remind you. And, as I've told you before, I might find a way of getting what I want without words. There are more effective means than talking.'

'You—you'd compromise me in some way?'

His hands tightened on her trembling shoulders, a flash of anger in his eyes. 'That's an old-fashioned way of putting it.'

'I'm an old-fashioned girl, remember.'

'And, considering the mother who reared you, very undisciplined.'

'That doesn't answer my question,' she whispered, so oddly breathless she might have been running.

'We'll see.' His eyes glittered as they travelled slowly over her fragile young beauty. As though drawn near the edge of endurance, he said harshly, 'I want you,

Alex, and I confess I don't want to wait. I want you in my bed, to make love to you until you hadn't one thought left in that crazy little head of yours, other than to want to belong to me. One of these days, with or without a wedding ring, I might be tempted—if you try me too far.'

Her legs went so weak she couldn't retreat when his hand slid down to her breast. 'A habit of mine,' without mirth he noted her nervous agitation. 'Why does your heart race when I touch you? I've never known such instant response.'

'It can only be hate,' she cried, ignoring the protesting strength of her love.

'I don't have to believe it,' he taunted, but letting her go. 'You look all eyes, worn out. I'd advise a good rest before dinner.'

'That's the last thing . . .' Alex began.

'Suit yourself,' his mouth compressed. 'I have enough to do without wasting time and sympathy on those who don't want it.'

She prayed he would go but, contrarily, had to stop him. 'I was led to believe you never spent any time here.'

'I haven't spent a lot,' his dark eyes were very steady, 'but I have you to consider now, and my own inclinations. From now on I'll be here most of the year. Every year.'

'You won't find other distractions so easily, not in the Outback.'

'If by that,' he said coolly, 'you mean other women, I won't need them. Not if I have you.'

'You take too much for granted!'

'I did use the word if.'

'How gracious of you!' Her satin-smooth face lifted defiantly, while conversely she struggled with a compulsion to cling to him, her mouth suddenly yearning for his kiss. It had been four days . . . Strangely shaken, she asked, 'How long do I have?'

'Until I can't stand any more.' He turned away, coldly arrogant, only a faint tinge of red under the hardness of his jaw betraying him. 'Right now I'm going out to the mustering camp. I might see you at dinner.'

When he had gone, Alex went numbly to the bed, drawn irresistibly to the powerful shape of him, still imposed on the covers. Weakly she dropped down to it, curving her head to the exact indentation of his on the pillow. 'Until he couldn't stand any more,' he had said, without stopping to consider anyone else! Her hands clenched, her body stiffened as erotic sensation seemed to strike up from where he had lain, enveloping her in a wave of excruciating desire. Shamefully she realised it wouldn't take much to have her rushing after him, begging him to make love to her.

Blindly ready to capitulate, she was about to scramble off the bed and catch him up when suddenly she fell back in an anguished little heap. It was no use. For all he wanted her, hadn't he made it quite clear that she bored him? Hadn't he spoken of it emphatically to Ruby? Nor had he ever pretended he was in love. Stricken, Alex stayed where she was. Nothing could provide a better antidote than that. She should be thankful she had remembered in time, before she had lost her head completely.

During the next few days Chase kept his promise to leave her alone. Most of the time he was out with his men, mustering cattle, or busy in the yards around the homestead. Alex caught occasional glimpses of him, dressed for the job in checked shirts and khaki drill trousers, standing well over six foot in his high-heeled elastic-sided boots. He might have been away from Coolabra for long spells, but he was still the Boss, still able to take absolute control, an authority on everything. And there was no doubt in anyone's mind that the respect he commanded went far beyond the actual boundaries of the station.

Alex avoided asking questions herself, but couldn't

prevent herself from listening when her mother asked them. Aunt Harriet was usually quite co-operative, never loath to talk of her beloved nephew. The information thus gathered so obviously impressed Enid that Alex shivered, fearing to even try to define her own feelings. It was better not to. Why pretend to be brave? It was much more comfortable to continue in a state of numb indifference than to expose herself to unnecessary pain.

Chase wasn't always at a distance, however. He was there at dinner, always the perfect host, distinguished in perfectly cut dark lounge suits which bore no resemblance to the dust-covered attire he wore during the day. The evenings were something Alex looked forward to. Drew Blake usually joined them, along with two young jackaroos who were gaining experience to run stations of their own, and twice visitors dropped in.

Yes, the evenings were fun, Alex had to admit, not too surprised that her mother helped to make them so. Enid had social flair, she was also beautiful, and Alex suddenly realised she was not all that much older than Chase. Once, catching them laughing together, she saw Enid wasn't really out of his generation at all, and was startled by a hot thrust of jealousy. It was amazing how a domineering woman like her mother could be so easily subdued by a little charm. Without trying, Chase seemed able to do just that.

When he could spare the time he took Alex and Enid out riding. Enid was an excellent horsewoman, something Chase appeared to appreciate. It was generally the two of them who led the way, leaving Alex to trail behind. She didn't mind this so much—it did afford her an opportunity to study Chase unobserved, which she often found herself doing to the exclusion of everything else. The sight of him was becoming necessary to her, though she would rather have died than that he should know it!

She felt almost pleased when, one day when they were out, Enid proclaimed that while she was enjoying her visit, as a permanent residence Coolabra would be too lonely for her.

Alex, before Chase could speak, found herself very much on the defensive. 'I haven't noticed any loneliness, Mother. There's always something going on, and to do. It's really wonderful. I love it!'

No sooner had she spoken than she wished she hadn't. Chase's face wore a look of deep satisfaction. Recklessly Alex dug her heels in the sides of the lovely little mare she rode, feeling, as she always did when he looked at her intently, a need to escape. Yet his sharp, taunting smile that followed her mocked her ability ever to do so completely!

One afternoon, after he had been home five days, he announced that he was going to Mount Isa.

'Oh, then you must take Alex,' his aunt exclaimed, 'She would liked to have gone while you were in Sydney, but no one had time to take her.'

'So I believe,' he drawled, his eyes veiled. 'That was unfortunate. Do you still have—urgent shopping to do, Alex?'

He knew why she had wanted to go and her cheeks burned. She had no doubts, now, that he had left precise orders that she wasn't to leave the station. 'Yes, I still have shopping to do,' she smiled, determined to annoy by defying him. It was later in the day than he usually made such a trip. He would be in a hurry, and if her presence proved an irritant, so much the better. It would make him think twice, in future, before making offers he didn't expect to have taken up. And about keeping her a virtual prisoner!

'It will be my pleasure,' he smiled dryly, startling her. 'You can run and get your hat while I have a word with these two ladies.'

Not thinking anything of this, she did as she was

told. She noticed he hadn't asked her mother. Of course Enid never liked flying, so she wouldn't have come anyway, and Chase knew this. Her pleasure fading a little, Alex didn't hurry so fast upstairs. These days he appeared to be studying Enid's comfort more than her own.

Unable to resist it, Alex hinted at this as they flew out from the station. 'You don't have to try so hard with Mother, Chase. She loves you already. Or rather what you stand for.'

'One day soon,' he muttered laconically, 'I might just strangle you.'

'A girl needs something to look forward to,' she said coolly.

'I'm sure I can do better than that.' His hands tightened on the controls as though he doubted it.

'Surprise me?' she suggested sarcastically. 'I've already had one sample!'

'You think I couldn't?'

She didn't care for the slight note of menace but felt superbly confident, in her present position. He couldn't do much more than threaten while handling a plane. Chase might look like a pirate, but he was fundamentally a gentleman. That much she believed. He would never do anything to totally embarrass her.

They lapsed into a rather taut silence. Then he asked, 'Are you dead set on Mount Isa, Alex?'

'Not really.' Her beautifully slender brows drew together. 'I like it. Why?'

'I was thinking of taking you to Alice. It would make a change.'

'Alice Springs?'

He nodded. 'You've never been. You can't leave without at least one visit.'

That hurt somehow. Quickly, to hide the feeling of being punched in the stomach, she faltered, 'Haven't you left it rather late in the day?'

Indifferently he shrugged. 'There's enough time to get there and back. We don't have to stay long.'

'How about your business in Mount Isa?'

'I can do it in Alice.'

'If you like, then.' She felt a stir of anticipation. Most people in the world had heard of Alice Springs. It must be surprising that every Australian hadn't been there.

He changed direction with the minimum of effort. 'We won't have time to have a proper look at places like Ayers Rock, but we might fly over it. Another day I'll take you.'

One minute he talked of her leaving, the next as if she was here to stay. Moodily she glanced sideways at the strength of his rugged profile, then she tried to relax, watching his smooth competence with the plane. There was a yearning inside her to know what he was really thinking. How could she feel secure until she knew what he thought? He might have shown her many things about herself, but, to her, he still remained a mystery.

The drone of the engines combined with the heat of the sun to send her to sleep. Her body slumped bonelessly as her heavy lashes curved to her cheeks. The sky above them was blue, the earth below red, the distances immense. There was nothing to stop her slipping over the edge into dreamland.

The terseness of Chase's voice, when it woke her, came as something of a shock. They had been flying for some time, making south-west.

'Alex, wake up! We're going down.'

'Down?' Dragged from unconsciousness, she took a second to realise where she was, but she had too much faith in Chase to panic. The engines spluttered, as though they had been jerked, but she had heard engines spluttering in planes before and seen them right themselves. There were seldom disastrous consequences. Yet

Chase looked grim. Her eyes widened on his face.

'What's wrong?'

'I wish to God I knew. Keep your safety belt on and shut up, there's a good girl. I'm doing my damnedest.'

She wished she was as cool as he was. She was unable to stay silent. After checking her belt she persisted nervously, 'Haven't you any idea what's wrong?'

'At a guess, petrol. The gauge hasn't been moving. A plane isn't a car, though. We can't stop and take a look.'

The engines roared to life again and her hopes simultaneously soared. 'Does this happen often?' she gasped.

'I hope not,' he muttered, in deep concentration, which she saw was justified as the engines cut completely and they glided towards the ground.

'Do as I told you!' he shouted. 'I'm trying to radio our position and I don't have much time.'

'Chase!' she cried, her voice rising as the plane seemed to glide at an alarming rate towards the burnt red earth. 'I'm sorry——' Quickly ashamed, her voice fell to a whisper which she was sure he didn't hear. The air was rushing by, making a peculiar high whining noise in the wings, without any competition from the engines. The sound was eerie, filling her with dread.

'Keep your belt on,' Chase was shouting, 'when we hit the ground. Don't release it until we stop or you'll be thrown. Then get out fast. Understood?'

'What about you?' The fear she felt was for him, not herself. She wished he knew.

'I'll be right behind you.' A quick glance showed his approval of her control and she felt curiously comforted. 'Good girl!'

The country beneath them was flat. Then she became aware of patches of trees, of gullies gouged from the red rock between rugged outcrops on which a plane might easily be smashed. Urgently she wanted to ask if they were still on Coolabra, but had more sense than to bother Chase now. He looked cool, he obviously knew what he was doing, but he had to get the most out of each uplifting current of air to reach the flatter ground ahead.

Let him make it, she prayed, her eyes clinging to him, wanting to tell him how much she loved him, when they might both be about to die, but unable to speak. Her voice was lost and she couldn't find it, as the breath was drawn rapidly from her taut body. The plane hit a flat piece of gravel, then bounced, straight into the side of a scrub-covered hillock. The shudder it gave in its last lurch was sickening and grinding, and Alex felt every bone in her body had been jolted.

Automatically her hands reached to follow Chase's instructions, but he was there, doing it for her. Swiftly he released her belt, almost flinging her from the wrecked plane. She heard the weight of him descending behind her.

'Run for it!' His voice was harsh as she scrambled clumsily to her feet. Petrol fumes were heavy on the air and she didn't need to be told he feared fire. Grabbing her arm, he dragged her along with him.

They hadn't gone far when the plane blew up, the heat and flames from it throwing them to the ground. 'Come on!' Chase pulled her to her feet again, after brief seconds. 'If we don't get out of here the heat will get us!'

There were trees ahead sheltering a creek, in which there was mercifully a little water. Alex could still feel the terrible heat from the plane as she sank down beside it. She would liked to have immersed herself in it, but she hadn't the strength. She felt sick.

'Take it easy,' Chase said tersely, looking closely at her, rather than the burning plane. He was pushing her thick hair from off her hot face, his hands going over her, making sure she was only suffering from fright. 'It could have been worse. We're still alive.'

'You think so?' she murmured bitterly, a lack of appreciation in her. She had a longing for sympathy, not bracing comments. She felt sick, her head was dizzy—which was strange, as she wasn't hurt.

Was Chase hurt? Her eyes suddenly anxious, ashamed that she had only been thinking of herself, she stared at him. 'Are you all right?'

'Yes,' he said briefly. 'We're both only shaken. I'll give you a couple of tablets and you'll feel better.'

'What about yourself?'

'I'll survive,' he said shortly, his eyes still closely on her, trying to assess the extent of shock. 'It's a golden rule in this part of the country, my darling.'

His last two words sent her more into shock than the plane crash. Tension and excitement whirled through her, causing colour to stain her white cheeks.

'You're becoming over-emotional.' His eyes darkened with concern, searching her disturbed young face. 'Try and relax.'

'Will anyone know where we are?' Alex dragged what seemed a sensible question from her suddenly chaotic thoughts.

'I transmitted our position, but it might take time. I doubt if we'll have any callers today.'

That didn't worry her immediately; there was nothing she could do about it. Intently she watched as he opened a pack. Aloud she wondered how he came to have it.

'It's a kind of survival kit. It can save lives.'

'What went wrong, Chase?'

'Hard to tell,' he flicked a quick frowning glance at the smouldering wreckage. 'It's not always easy to find out, either, not when the whole thing goes up in flames like that.' He was disinclined to say anything further and she didn't press him. His explanation was feasible and she knew little about planes, large or small, herself.

She took the tablets he offered obediently, not even protesting when he put his arm around her shoulders to help her sit up. Quickly she swallowed them, along with the lump in her throat, having a silly desire to turn her head into his shoulder and weep. She wanted to weep and cling to his strong, lean body, to have her face and mouth covered by kisses, which she assured herself would only be comforting.

She drew a steadying breath as he let her go with merely a brotherly pat on the shoulder he held. 'Will we have to stay here all night?' she asked shakily.

Chase studied her for a sharp moment, as though wondering how much she could take. Her apparent calmness appeared to convince him she was over the worst. 'I'm afraid so. It certainly wouldn't be wise to try to get anywhere on foot. You have to be patient, Alex. The territory's huge, but someone will eventually find us.'

Suddenly a thought struck her, making her heart thump erratically with shock. 'You did this on purpose, didn't you?' she burst out impetuously. 'Now you think I'll have to marry you after this, whether I want to or not!'

An expression of fury hardened his face, blazing from his dark eyes. His hands curled, as though he would liked to have used them on her slender neck, the force of his fury bringing him precipitately to his feet. 'You're out of your mind, Alex. It's probably delayed shock from the crash. I'd advise you to say nothing more until you feel better.'

'There's nothing wrong with me!' She believed this to be true, but her voice held the merest hint of terror. 'I could have been killed, though.'

'And you think I risked your life deliberately?' He had lost any urge to reason with her, for she saw only cold anger in his face.

Heedless of it, driven to a point where she didn't

seem able to stop, she rushed recklessly on. 'Why not? You said you'd find a way to compromise me. You're too much of an expert for an accident like this just to happen!'

His voice came so coldly it chilled. 'Go on,' he begged softly. 'Why stop there? It would be a shame.'

'I haven't anything more to say,' she gasped, clinging to a pathetic dignity.

'But I have, miss!' His fury became white-hot, lighting up his eyes with a strange brilliance. 'Do you honestly believe I would risk my life in order to marry a stupid little fool like you?'

'I—I wouldn't think for a moment you believed you were risking your life.'

'My God!' He stared down at her with deadly emphasis. 'So I was simply performing a huge stunt? Alex,' he controlled himself with an obvious effort, as she began convulsively to shiver, 'no one ever steps out of a crashed plane with any other thought in their head but that they're lucky to be alive. And no one is less than shocked to some extent. I suggest you forget what you've just accused me of. At least, say no more about it. You'll only regret it, once you've had time to pull yourself together.'

CHAPTER NINE

UNHAPPPILY, Alex looked away from him. Her pride
made her want to resist his advice, but she dared not.
She had a terrible suspicion that she had made a fool of
herself and might never be forgiven. She had to have
time to think things out—and by the look of it, Chase's
face particularly, she was going to have plenty! Hours
on her own, to contemplate her own foolish indiscre-
tions.

'I'm sorry,' she whispered, altogether defeated.

'Forget it.' She didn't notice his frowning glance on
the tears which slid down her enchanting profile. He
made no attempt to supply comfort, which might have
been too soon after the bitter words they had exchanged. Besides, everyone knew the therapeutic value
of tears. With an oddly suppressed sigh he left her, to
begin gathering leaves and sticks for a fire, the set of his
mouth indicating that his mind wasn't wholly on the
job he was doing.

Furtively, after a few minutes, Alex scrubbed away
her tears and watched him. His movements were quick
and methodical, surprising her. In no time at all he was
serving her with tea brewed up in a billycan. It had a
taste all of its own and she drank it gratefully.

The tea revived her, steadying her nerves. Even so,
she found it difficult to look at him. Much as she tried,
she could not meet his eyes. She felt better but kept her
fair head bent over her cup, quite at a loss as to how
she might bridge the awful chasm of silence between
them. It must be up to her, but for the life of her she
didn't know where to begin.

Chase, dryly aware of this, gave her half a bar of

chocolate. 'I'll have to see if I can find a fish in the creek for dinner,' he said lightly.

Hoping, from his change of tone, that she was forgiven, she glanced up quickly. 'Are there any fish?'

'We might be lucky.' He examined her uplifted face grimly. 'Stay where you are until I come back. I won't be long, but don't move from where you're sitting.'

She obeyed, but watched his tall figure until he was out of sight. For the first time since coming to northern Australia she felt lonely. At the homestead there was always so much going on, she never had time to feel lonely, but this was different—quite different. Even out riding on her own she had never felt lost as she did now. Of course, she reminded herself, that was what Chase and she were—lost! Possibly hundreds of miles away from anywhere. Which perhaps explained why her thoughts were so anxious.

When Chase returned she had to hide how relieved she was. 'Did you find any fish?' she asked politely.

'Yes,' he smiled, just a twist of his lips but a smile of sorts. 'There's deeper water further along the creek, I've discovered, if you'd like to bathe.'

Alex was hot and sticky, the thin sundress, which was all she wore, clinging to her. It would be lovely if she could. Her eyes lit up, then clouded. 'We haven't a towel, though? Or a change of clothing.'

He laughed, clearly relieved by her eagerness. 'There's a small towel in the kit, if you must, but you'll soon dry. I'm afraid there's nothing we can do about anything else.'

'Shall I go first?' She glanced at him uncertainly.

Again he laughed, seeming in an altogether better humour. 'We'll go in together.'

So this was why he was smiling. 'Oh, no, we won't!' she exclaimed. 'If you . . .'

'Listen to me, Alex,' he cut in sardonically, refusing to argue. 'This is no time for false modesty. You've just been through a harrowing experience and you can't take risks. Either I come with you or you stay here, just as you please. I'm sure what you're wearing under your dress will be as adequate as some of the swimming gear I've seen you in.'

The water was wonderfully refreshing, and Alex swam in her bra and panties while Chase, because of the promise he had wryly made, sat on the bank and didn't look. Because he was so near she felt oddly strung up, and she hurried so he might have his turn before dark. There was also the fish to catch, but she didn't know how he was going to manage to do all that.

Her thin underclothing clung but dried easily in a few minutes. Quickly she slipped back into her dress. Her dress was thin, too, and she wished she had brought a coat. She shivered to think what the night was going to be like without even one blanket between them.

An hour later, as she sat under the trees again, watching him expertly cooking their supper, she considered her former doubts ironically. Chase Marshall appeared able to accomplish anything he set out to do very easily. While the fish baked, wrapped in leaves, he explained conversationally that the creek was full of them.

'Some of the established waterholes are.'

'You caught them very quickly.' She didn't pretend to be anything but impressed.

The heart of the fire was glowing hot and he viewed it with satisfaction. 'I used a trick an old Aborigine taught me, when I was a boy. They eat a lot of fish when they can get it.'

It was too difficult to imagine Chase that young. Alex gave up and came to the fire. He had his sleeves rolled up, his powerful arms brown and sinewy. Quickly she looked away. 'I'll take over, if you like,' she offered. 'You must want a rest.'

Coming lithely up beside her from a crouching position, he taunted, 'How easily your feelings change from hate to love. It can't be comfortable.'

'Why should love or hate come into it?' she retorted, stung by his sarcasm. 'I'm simply offering to pull my weight.'

'Don't be over-generous,' he drawled. 'There's not that much of it. Anyway, our supper's almost ready. All you have to do is enjoy it.'

She did enjoy it, in spite of his jibes. They had no plates and ate with their fingers, but Alex couldn't remember tasting anything so delicious. The light went as they finished. 'Just as well there's no washing up to do.' She tried to speak casually.

He glanced at her quickly. 'All we can do now is sleep. No one's going to find us in the dark.'

'I've been listening for a plane ever since we crashed,' she said.

'You think I haven't?'

'I'm sorry,' she apologised helplessly, realising he wouldn't miss a thing. 'I keep thinking of the worry we must be causing. Your aunt, my parents—they won't know whether we're dead or alive.'

'They won't lose their heads, you know,' he said calmly. 'Harriet never gives up hope easily. She'll be able to reassure your mother.'

'But what will they be thinking?' Her choked exclamation was bitter as she spread out her slim hands despairingly.

'I wondered when you'd get round to it,' Chase said grimly, his teeth white in the darkness as he snapped them together. 'I suppose you've even gone into the big seduction scene?'

'You're hateful!' she cried, anger sparkling in her huge eyes. 'Of course I haven't! It's just—well,' her voice faltered unsteadily, 'I've never been in a situation like this before.'

'You think I have?' His eyes flashed with suppressed violence. He glared down at her, his hands coming out to bite into her shoulders. Then suddenly he relaxed, taking pity on her. 'Alex, listen to me! I wasn't going to mention this now, but maybe it might help. Before we left I told both your mother and Harriet we might have some news for them when we returned.'

'News?'

'Our engagement.'

'I don't believe it!' The breath seemed driven from her body at such presumption. 'What made you so confident?'

'A hunch I had.' As he met her incredulous gaze, his voice hardened, 'I've seen your pining little glances when you thought I wasn't looking and I suddenly decided to make up your mind for you. If uncertainty doesn't do anything for you, it does damn all for me.'

'It's not true!' Alex could barely control her agitation. 'I think you're making it up!'

'You might believe me if I show you this.' His eyes were derisive as he drew a ring from his breast pocket— a sapphire, diamond and platinum ring, a glittering thing of priceless beauty. 'The stones match your eyes,' he said. 'It wasn't meant for anyone else.'

A funny little gasp escaped Alex as she stared at it, the absolute perfection of it, grasped in his well shaped hand. She tried to imagine it on her finger and numbly shook her head. As Chase offered it, it seemed to symbolise a ball and chain, a loveless imprisonment from which she might never escape.

'If you accept this,' she heard him say calmly, 'you would make a lot of people happy, and save yourself a pile of misery.'

'What good reasons for becoming engaged!' Her laughter was brief and scornful. 'Does it matter how I feel?'

'I think so.'

'Some might think we're having an orgy out here, but

I'm sure not everyone will believe it,' she replied bitterly. ,

'Humiliation can be hard to take.' He regarded the ring consideringly, forcing her to do the same. 'You have others to think of, Alex, apart from yourself. I'd advise you to think it over.'

'I don't need to.'

'So you refuse to wear my ring?'

'No.' She had to keep it short or she might burst into tears of misery. 'Keep it for a girl who'll appreciate you.'

'I might at that,' he drawled harshly. 'After all, my primary motivation was to provide Coolabra with an heir.'

Alex pretended to yawn, while her heart went cold with yearning. She would have given him anything he wanted! Now there was nothing left between them, not even to talk about. 'Where do I sleep?' she whispered, doubting she ever would.

'Over here.' Replacing the ring in his pocket, without any obvious regret, Chase guided her to a rough shelter of bark and branches. Earlier she had seen him erecting it, but hadn't allowed herself to wonder.

Nervously she pulled back. 'I can't sleep there!'

'We both will.'

'You as well?' She began to tremble. 'Chase—it's not possible . . .'

Impatiently he jerked her forward, under the crudely formed canopy of leaves. 'I think, girl, it's about time you faced facts. Up till now you've been courageous, so don't spoil your record. It could be days before we're found. I hope not, but it could be. Sleeping out in the open, without so much as a jacket between us, could be fatal. The nights are too cold. Even this shelter might not be enough.'

'The fire?' she protested feebly.

'Fine, if you have a blanket and are prepared to stay

awake indefinitely to keep it going. Unfortunately I'm
no natural hero, Alex. I'll gamble higher on our chances
of survival if we keep together.'

So mixed up she couldn't think straight, Alex
frowned. The night was dark—there was no moon to
explain the mysterious rustling sounds in the nearby
undergrowth. In the distance a wild dingo howled,
making a coward of her. 'I suppose so,' she agreed
numbly.

It was no more than a rough construction that closed
about her uncomfortably as she crawled inside. Chase
followed and lay down. Quite impersonally he put an
arm around her, dragging her down to him. 'Stop fighting,' he said curtly, his hand on her bare arm. 'You're
half frozen already.'

Alex numbled something neither of them understood.
She was half frozen, but with fear more than cold, the
fear being not so much of Chase as of her own feelings.
At any time, when he was around, she found them difficult to control. How was she to manage them in this
impossible situation?

Already the heat from his body was beginning to
warm her, as was the arm he was rubbing gently with
the flat of his hand. Her head lay where he had pulled
it, against his shoulder, she could feel his heart beating
heavily under her cheek. The rise and fall of it should
have sent her to sleep, but because of it she couldn't
forget he was there.

His hand left her arm and settled on her hair, his
fingers pushing gently through the tangled strands,
smoothing it off her ears, away from her nape, from her
bare shoulders. His hands made soothing, circling
movements, relaxing her, to begin with, as if he
intended they should.

She felt her body weakening, but her mouth went
curiously dry. She couldn't even pretend to be asleep.
To break the silence, which was rapidly becoming taut,

she asked, 'Do Aborigines really sleep in a shelter like this, Chase?'

He nodded slowly, his mind not completely on the subject. 'Some of them still do.'

'However do they manage?'

'Probably much as we're doing now.' His voice was deliberately teasing. 'Many of them never wear clothes, yet they never feel the cold.'

'We aren't wearing all that much ourselves,' she reminded him, then wished she had never mentioned the subject. Chase was so near she could feel every hard muscle as he stretched out beside her. 'I don't think we need be as close as this, Chase.' She tried to edge away, surprised at her own reluctance.

'Yes, we do,' he said curtly. 'And you can believe I'm more uncomfortable than you are.'

She flushed, hoping he didn't feel the heat in her face as it rested against him. Her senses stirred, her breathing quickened as her hand went defensively to her hot cheeks.

As he spoke he sighed, turning restlessly on to his back, and the hand she raised was caught on the hair-roughened skin of his chest. The tips of her fingers were immediately sensitive to the sparks of electricity she found there. Her breath sucked in. Curiously riveted, her sudden panic fading, she allowed herself to explore the muscled contours which tensed beneath her slow voyage of discovery.

She didn't think of it as being in any way provocative, although every intimate thought she had ever had about Chase rushed through her head in a chaotic torrent. She could feel the thunderous beating of his heart under her palm and pressed down on it experimentally.

When he stopped her, her eyes went automatically to his, wide and questioning. 'Chase——' she began uncertainly, shocked by the frank sensuality she saw there. It jerked her out of her present stupor, but into one infinitely worse.

Mutely he shook his head, without words, sensing her paralysing awareness. There was a look of self-derision on his face, yet mixed with torment. 'God, Alex,' he muttered with a groan, and all her fine talk of rejection counted for nothing against the consuming desire of his lips.

Wildly she opened her mouth to protest, but her senses spun from the demanding ecstasy of his touch and she could do nothing. Her head swam, and now it was the turn of his hands. She could feel them on her savagely, holding her to him, sliding down her back to her hips, clenching on her spine, as though he was keeping a tiger at bay.

Her face was pressed against his chest now and she could feel his tongue seeking out the hollows of her cheek and neck. Darkness, full of the feel of him, made coherent thought impossible and a dizzying weakness spread through her limbs. Then his mouth was on hers again and he was crushing her passionately against the hardening muscles of his body.

'Alex?' his voice came urgently as his head lifted, his breath harsh on her face, 'Alex, listen to me. Have you thought any more about marrying me?'

Not entirely conscious, she gasped, 'Please don't talk, Chase. I don't want to.' She wanted nothing that might destroy the intimacy between them. Her blood was a churning whirlpool of feeling, whipped to a frenzy by his tortured breathing. Words could only spoil whatever this thing was between them. Talk could only drag her back to cold reality and she would rather stay in this enchanting world of the senses. Trying to convey this silently, she placed her hands on his face, her fingers lingering on the hard bones before pushing upwards into his dark hair. 'Kiss me, darling,' she implored, never too proud to beg.

'Alex! For pity's sake!' His hands caught her, gripped her, thrusting her away from him.

Her eyes, suddenly wide and startled, sought his, and

she could actually see the physical control he was exerting. He sat up and away from her, shaking his head disbelievingly. 'I guess this wasn't such a good idea, after all.'

Alex drew a deep breath, endeavouring to recover her composure. It wasn't easy, she felt completely shattered. She had been in Chase's arms before but had never felt as terrible as this. Recalling her own wanton response, she shivered, averting her eyes from the taut stillness of his figure.

He wasn't accusing her of anything, but he had been the one to call a halt. If only she had been the one to draw back. Now he could taunt her for ever and she had no defence.

There seemed nothing to say. Feeling taut as a bowstring, she heard him mutter something under his breath. She didn't need to look at him; she could sense his grimness.

'Try to sleep.' He stood up. 'I'll go and replenish the fire.'

He meant he hoped she would be alseep when he came back. Knowing this, Alex didn't fight the wave of exhaustion that swept over her. In Chase's arms she had been brought wholly alive, but now he had gone all her vitality disappeared. She watched him walk to the fire, pick up some brushwood and throw it on. He dusted his hands, then stood staring at it. Alex's eyes grew heavy watching. She didn't remember falling asleep.

In the early dawn she woke, sleepily whispering his name. He wasn't there. Where could he be? Full recall came suddenly, bringing shock. She remembered him standing by the fire, etched darkly against the flames, but had fallen asleep with no recollection of where he had gone.

Panic forced limbs, stiff from cold and a hard bed, to action, tearing her from the primitive shelter. 'Chase!' her voice came hoarsely, but loud enough for him to have heard, had he been around. There was no answer, no sign of him!

'Chase!' she cried again, and again only silence answered her anguished appeal. Where was he? Had he slept by the campfire and wandered off in a befuddled state of mind? Vague recollections of the things she had heard could happen in the Outback struck terror into her. The trauma of the plane-crash might have affected Chase, too. She would never believe he would do anything foolish when completely in control of his senses, but temporarily deprived of them he could have fallen foul of many things. Only a fool would be unaware of the dangers that lurked in such a wild country at night.

She was even more horror-stricken to realise suddenly that Chase's shirt was draped over her shoulders. If she was warm, he must be nearly frozen! The creek? She would go to the creek first. He might be gathering wood. Leaving the smouldering fire and the white towel flag he had erected on a makeshift flagpole, she ran in that direction.

He wasn't there. Breathlessly Alex ran on, the absolute silence mocking her, until she came to the deeper pools, the one where they had bathed the night before. Chase was there. He had been swimming, for his hair was damp, and he had obviously pulled on his pants in a hurry, because patches of wet were coming through.

In her relief Alex was so angry she didn't stop to think. 'How dared you frighten me like this!' she cried, her small face scarlet as she ran to him, her hands clenched to tight little fists to pound his broad chest. 'I hate you, Chase Marshall! You're a monster!' In her fury she forgot about the sacrifice he had made of his shirt. 'You're the most selfish, egocentric man I ever met!'

The welcoming smile on his face faded. 'Shut up, Alex!'

'I won't! I'm sick of being told to shut up. I——'

Before she could get out another word, he caught hold of her. 'Why waste breath?' he mocked. 'This could be more effective...' without pausing he lifted her, throwing her ruthlessly in the deepest part of the pool, 'and what you've had coming for a long time,' he shouted tersely, as she sank like a stone.

She came up spluttering, full of creek water, half drowning. 'And no more than you deserve!' Chase added, lowering himself to the grassy bank, to watch her.

'Oh ...' Unfortunately she sank again, before she could even start on the tirade that was shooting around her head like red hot fireworks, waiting to be released. A necessity to breathe was the only inclination to survive the second immersion.

As Chase sat on the bank, considering her closely, she struck out blindly for the shore. Reaching it, she dragged her sodden body from the murky water. She must have gone deep as she seemed to have stirred up all the mud from the bottom. Wild with despairing distaste, she began wrenching off her dress. Water poured from it, mixed with red mud. She was half drowned, choking, her fury still red-hot, so she was scarcely aware of what she was doing.

Chase's smothered laughter infuriated her further. Buttons flew until her dress fell in a wet heap at her feet. Then she gasped, realising, to her consternation, that she was almost naked. 'Oh, no!' she cried helplessly, flinging back her streaming hair and beginning to weep.

'Alex!' Immediately he was on his feet, completely sober, taking charge of her. 'Don't take on so, girl. Maybe we both needed that.'

'Speak for yourself!' she gulped bitterly.

'For both of us,' he insisted firmly.

'I—I thought you were lost, that you might be hurt,' she sobbed, quite unable to pull herself together.

'Did you?' he said, thoughtful about that. Then, whimsically, 'I simply intended having the bathroom first. If I'd had anything to write with I'd have left you a note.'

'Don't joke about it, Chase!' Refusing to be so easily appeased, she stamped her small foot.

'Perhaps our sense of humour isn't up to it,' he agreed, offering her a large white handkerchief. 'Here, take this. I was keeping it for emergencies, but this might just rate as one.'

She tried to grasp it, but her hands were shaking too badly.

'Let me,' he sighed wryly.

Blindly obedient, Alex turned fully to him, too muddled to think and barely noticing his hands dry the water from her face and shoulders. His steady movements were soothing and she didn't see the sudden blaze of desire in his eyes.

Her lashes felt weighted, her eyes almost drowsily closed when she felt his hands tense and his mouth drop to her lightly tanned throat. 'Alex,' he groaned, his mouth hot against her skin, 'you're beautiful.'

Beautiful? How could she be, half drowned as she was in creek water? Colour flooded her cheeks as she remembered her state of semi-nakedness, that she had nothing on but her thin panties and bra.

Chase bent her head back, his mouth moving up the slender column of her neck to crush her lips, his eyes alight and burning. 'Don't fight me,' he growled.

Immediately she came to her senses. He was kissing her with a bruising intensity, seemingly uncaring that he hurt her. Frightened, she tried to struggle, but he would not release her. By coming here this morning she appeared to have released a storm of feeling he could no longer control. Last night had been but a prelude to the avalanche of savage passion that descended on her now. Under his mouth she gave a half sob, the tenseness of her body pleading with him.

He drew a shaken breath, his arms slackening, as if striving for composure. With a gasp Alex stumbled away from him, but moving too quickly she fell. The sun was already on the sandy grass. Yesterday's heat, being still trapped in it, warmed her as she lay helpless before him.

Chase knelt down beside her, turning her over gently. The clean fresh scent of him hit her somewhere in her stomach, making her legs curl.

'Darling,' he said thickly, 'I would never hurt you.'

She looked at him, realising the longer he held her the less was her desire for escape. When she didn't move he began kissing her again, as if he couldn't help himself, and after a moment she relaxed, the pressure of his mouth obliterating everything else, the touch of his hands sensually arousing.

Surrendering to the strength of her own feelings, Alex put her arms around his neck, arching her slender body against his. Between them there sprang to life a sudden urgency. She began returning his kisses eagerly, her hands trembling as much as his, her breath shuddering.

Beneath the insistent pressure of his mouth her own parted with a helpless cry, admitting his passion. His breath was as ragged as hers as his lips burned over her, pillaging her face and throat, and, when his hand thrust her flimsy bra aside, the throbbing fullness of her breasts.

Alex went tense, quivering, her nails digging into the smooth skin of his shoulders, her emotions roused to such a pitch she could deny him nothing. She opened glazed eyes, seeing, in odd wonder, his darkly flushed face. Chase moved restlessly, as if desire was building up in him a kind of agony. His breath was hot and rasping on her face, his hands moved tentatively to her narrow hips, tightening over the warm curve of flesh he found there.

Urgently he groaned against her soft mouth, 'I want you, my darling, but I don't want to hurt you.'

He might have been giving her a last chance to go, but she was past all caring, only aware she could no longer refuse him, whatever he wanted. Her entire body was on fire with a need as great as his own.

When his control went, she found herself melting, her fears fading, utterly pliable as he pressed savagely down on her. There was her startled, whimpering cry at the beginning of pain—then, suddenly, an explosion of noise, roaring from the sky above them, thrusting them immediately apart.

It was a helicopter. Dimly Alex realised this almost before she heard Chase's harsh exclamation. When she opened dazed eyes he was already on his feet, away from her.

'They've found us, Alex.' For a second he stood quite still, his broad shoulders rigid, then, without looking at her, he strode from the protective cover of the trees which lined the creek. 'They're coming down beside the plane,' he called back.

Alex was hurrying to tidy herself up as best as she could with a mind still numb and butterflies dancing in her stomach. Feelings of shame were storming over her. The helicopter had saved her in more ways than one, she supposed, but if she'd used her common sense it shouldn't have been necessary. How could she have let her feelings run away with her to such an extent? Another moment—her cheeks colouring painfully, she remembered.

Managing to pull herself together, she stared with dismay at her ruined dress. It would be difficult to put back on. If she did manage to do it, she couldn't imagine what she would look like in it. 'What am I to do, Chase?' she cried, cold with embarrassment.

A quick glance, which she felt though did not see, told her he understood. 'Stay there while I fetch a rug.

They're sure to have one.'

'But—what will they think?' Wildly anxious, her eyes rose at last to his face, seeing in confusion how grim he was. His face was grey, his eyes bleak, and his mouth seemed to have a harsh ring around it.

'If they're my men, which I'm almost certain they will be, they aren't paid to think, Alex.'

She heard his breath released on a note of hard impatience, which might have been because of her. Her nervous reactions obviously irritated him. Any other girl might have been dancing about his feet, throwing her arms around him, instead of cowering here, shivering over something that had never even happened. She couldn't even find the courage to say she was glad they had been rescued.

No more than five minutes later Chase was back, carrying, of all things, a pair of jeans and a sweater. 'It's Drew all right,' he said. 'And Harriet sent you these. She remembered you were only wearing a thin dress that might not have survived an accident. Anyway, these are more practical.'

Gratefully she took them, but her voice was still frozen as she thanked him. Her hands seemed frozen, too, as she struggled into the jeans and fumbled clumsily with the zip.

'Can I help you?' She was so bemused she forgot he was standing watching her awkward efforts. His tone was somehow so intimate she coloured faintly. 'Oh, no, thank you,' she replied, catching her finger and wincing painfully.

With a terse snap of his white teeth Chase thrust her hands away, completing the job for her. When she gasped he seemed less intent on her slender body than the extreme whiteness of her face. 'For God's sake, Alex, you don't have to look so injured! Nothing happened.'

'Not your fault!' she muttered fiercely, near choking

as he swept the warm sweater over her head. His way of dressing her being suddenly less than gentle, she felt injured.

'I might be willing to take all the blame, if it will make you feel any better.'

She retorted wildly, her voice rising on a sob, 'I don't think I'll ever feel better again!'

Hurtfully he grasped her thin arms. 'Alex, listen to me! Drew's here—another chopper is coming. You're going to be surrounded. You'll have to pull yourself together.'

'I thought it didn't matter what your men thought,' she gasped. 'And I didn't know I was out of control.'

'You're tottering on the brink.' His eyes glittered coldly, showing no sympathy. 'It won't do, Alex. You know that.'

'I'm sorry.' She looked down at the ground and, as he let her go, bent to pick up her dress. 'I promise to behave. I won't do anything to ruffle your feelings.' As he appeared to think this unworthy of an answer, she said bitterly, 'They took their time getting here, didn't they?'

He wouldn't allow this. 'You realise we might not have been found for days?'

'Think how bored you would have been!'

Again his hand curled around her arm, his fingers like steel. 'Alex, I know you've been through a lot, but acting like a child won't solve anything. You have to think of others.'

'Who?' she burst out bitterly.

He sighed, his mouth compressed. 'Your parents, for instance.'

'Mother?'

'Your father, too. He's on his way, apparently. They sent for him.'

'But why?' Her eyes widened, swinging to his in angry despair.

'Why not?' He sounded as if he was holding his temper on a tight rein. 'Your mother did the right thing. She had to consider that you're his child, too. If we'd been killed he might never have forgiven her if she hadn't sent for him.'

'Will he be there when we get back?' she whispered, her face ashen.

'He could be.' Chase's eyes narrowed sharply. 'Or very shortly afterwards. Why?'

Mutely, Alex shook his head. All at once she couldn't bear it. No matter which way she looked she could only see rows of curious faces. They would all be wondering how Chase and she had spent the night. The question would be there, whether it was in their eyes or at the back of their minds. Without some kind of support she couldn't face it!

She glanced at Chase swiftly, flushing painfully, her mouth trembling as she saw the coldness of his expression. It took a lot of courage to ask. Her voice shook and she had to swallow twice. She might have given up, but it seemed imperative. Especially as her father might be there.

'Chase,' she whispered at last, 'may I wear your ring, please?'

CHAPTER TEN

'AH, the ring!' A flicker of surprise brought an odd smile to Chase's face which might have made Alex suspicious if she hadn't felt so distraught. Silently he searched for the ring in his pocket and held it in front of her. 'Give me your hand and I'll put it on.'

She shrank back while he gazed calmly down at her. Why, she wondered, wasn't he curious? Why wasn't he questioning her motives? Ordinarily he would have done, he was that kind of man. Weakly she faltered, 'It's not that sort of engagement.'

'How many sorts are there, for heaven's sake?' he asked softly, a conqueror, victory almost within his grasp, prepared to humour his victim.

'Chase, you know what manner of engagement this will be,' she stammered unhappily.

'Knowing what's between us, I thought I did,' he returned enigmatically, 'but I see you're going to use it merely to save your reputation.'

'Don't you think I need something, after this?' she cried desperately, not caring for the way his eyes darkened. 'You see, if Daddy's coming . . .'

'Ah, so it's Daddy's disapproval now, is it?'

'No . . .' Suddenly she felt very young, very tormented, very much at sea. 'Chase, you don't understand. Daddy isn't like that. He's never harassed me. He always had faith—always trusted me to do the right thing.'

'So you don't want to let him down?'

Sadly she shook her head. 'I don't know what he'll make of this, but at least it must make everything respectable.'

'If we're engaged, you mean?'

'Yes.' A deep sigh escaped her.

'Then stop worrying.' Tersely he watched her strained young face. 'When it suits me I can be as obliging as you like.' Before she could protest he caught her small hand in his big one and slipped the ring on her finger. Ignoring her murmur of alarm, he said mockingly, 'As it's the first time I've become engaged, I couldn't deprive myself of the pleasure. Who knows, it might be all I ever get!'

Stung, Alex snatched her hand away, her eyes riveted on the ring, her face white. 'I'm sure, after I've finished with it, Davina would appreciate it more!'

'I have no doubt.'

'Oh!' She stepped back as if he had struck her, forgetting the suggestion had been hers in the first place. But Chase followed up, taking a swift hold of her, 'All new engagements are surely sealed with a loving kiss?' he drawled, bending his head, without waiting for a reply, to crush her mutinous lips under his.

The internal fire was still there, fusing them but not comfortably. There were too many sparks, too much electricity. She felt scorched, burnt by his sudden harsh passion and her own too reckless response to it.

Fiercely she tore herself out of his arms, only to hear him say curtly, 'Suppose we go back now, before Drew comes looking for us.'

As she turned to stumble blindly alongside him, he added, 'They might have been here sooner if there hadn't been some doubt about the message I sent. You see, they all believed we'd gone to Mount Isa and thought I'd made a mistake. For as long as the light held yesterday, they searched in that direction. And another thing,' he paused sardonically, 'my aunt has already announced our engagement, believing, I imagine, she was doing the right thing.'

Drew immediately wished them well. 'A day late, I guess,' he smiled ruefully.

Coolly Chase acknowledged his congratulations, holding out Alex's thin hand. 'A day late for you, maybe, but I had the ring with me.'

Drew laughed appreciatively, never doubting for a moment Chase's genius for being one step ahead. If he appeared slightly stunned, his face only reflected the general feeling on the station. That Chase Marshall had been caught at last! By a lovely girl, but one who was surely too young to have been able to do it!

The ring, Alex saw, backed up Chase's story to the hilt—a not to be disputed fact.

Ruefully Drew said, 'Miss Harriet was in quite a state, as you can imagine. An air crash on top of an engagement was nearly too much for her.'

'Possibly, but she always keeps her head,' Chase said grimly.

'Always!' Drew agreed fervently, without realising his line of thought was slightly different from that of Chase's.

Alex understood exactly. It had all gone off with such precision it might have been planned by an expert. And of course that was what Chase was! She felt she might even be excused for believing he had contrived the crash deliberately. Nothing seemed beyond his capabilities.

She had thought it must be hours since the helicopter had arrived, but it had only been ten minutes. A further ten and the makeshift camp site was cleared and they were away. Word was relayed to Coolabra and to other people out searching. Congratulations and heartfelt relief winged back. To Alex, it seemed that the very air was delighted. It danced before her eyes as each message came across, dazzling her. She could find nothing to say, not even when Chase glanced at her anxiously. Silently she sat beside him, leaving him to talk to Drew. She noticed how they began discussing station business, as though nothing out of the ordinary had happened.

Her father was at Coolabra to welcome her home. They came down near the house and she stumbled to meet him. Regardless of Chase, she hugged him, tears in her eyes. 'It's so good to see you!' she whispered feverishly.

Her mother, along with Aunt Harriet and Mrs Young, were noticeably moved, and the whole thing might have developed into a flood of feminine tears if Chase had given them a chance. Almost at once he sent Alex upstairs with an attentive Mrs Young.

'A shower and bed, Mrs Young, I think. Alex is worn out.'

'But we must drink to your future happiness,' Aunt Harriet protested. 'The poor child does look tired, but I happen to know she's made of sterner stuff.'

'Not this time, I'm afraid. She's been through a lot.'

Chase overruled his aunt and Alex made her escape. Much as she would have liked to have stayed, especially to talk to her father, she would have found it impossible, and she suspected Chase knew it. Sometimes, she had to admit, his sensitivity amazed her. Not even her mother was allowed to accompany her. Chase took them all to his study and closed the door.

To her dismay, Alex not only fell asleep, but she slept the clock around. It was an uneasy sleep, during which she sensed the presence of someone often by her side. Once she fancied she felt hands on her hair, a low deep voice softly murmuring. Nothing was distinct, however, and next morning she was aghast to discover what the time was. Scarcely able to believe it, she dressed and rushed downstairs, to find everyone at breakfast.

Chase, looking tired, immediately rose to his feet as she ran through the door. 'Why didn't someone wake me?' she cried almost angrily, pulling out her usual chair.

It startled her a little when Chase said gently, 'No, not there, darling. Here, beside me,' but she hesitated only a moment before obeying him. She was even more surprised to find herself submitting weakly to his kiss before she sat down. The others would expect it, she thought bleakly, feeling the increased beat of her heart as his hard mouth descended.

She wasn't sure if it was her own ears, but his breathing seemed quite audible as he abruptly let her go. To hide it, she smiled at Aunt Harriet, then glanced from her mother to her father. He was looking much better this morning, his manner alert, his eyes bright.

'We had to celebrate your engagement without you,' he teased gently, after the chorus of enquiries regarding her health had died down.

'I'm sorry,' she wasn't sure whether she was or not, and felt unable to look at Chase, 'but there's plenty of time, surely?'

'I'm afraid I have to return to Sydney today,' he said wryly. 'I've an important conference tomorrow or I should certainly have accepted Chase's invitation to stay. What he showed me yesterday, when he wasn't attending to you, more than whetted my appetite. I sincerely hope he isn't about to saddle himself with a father-in-law he can't get rid of.'

The grin the two men exchanged over this proved they had taken to each other instantly, and Alex's spirits felt like lead.

'I think I'll come with you, Daddy, if you don't mind.'

A moment's silence was broken by her mother. 'I've decided to go back with your father, Alex, so there's no need for you to come, too.'

Chase didn't interrupt the conversation, but Alex noticed his hand clench tautly. 'It's not that,' she said stubbornly, 'I just think it would be better.'

Chase spoke at last, with the air of a man sore tried but willing to show tolerance. 'Would you rather be married in Sydney, Alex, after all?'

As though they had already discussed it! 'I'm not sure,' she said unsteadily. 'There's no hurry.'

Chase smiled around the table lightly, but his voice was terse. 'I'm in a hurry, but if Alex insists on going to Sydney today, it's all right by me. I'll come, too.'

Shaken by his decision, Alex had a wild presentiment of disaster. At loss for words, she stared at him, beginning slowly to realise what she might be up against.

'Alex,' Aunt Harriet grew alarmed, quite obviously loath to part with her, 'why not wait a little longer? Naturally, as your home is in Sydney, you might want to be married from there, but Chase isn't just any man, you know. There'll be a lot to arrange at Coolabra.'

'The wedding won't be for a while yet.' Alex bit her lip nervously, feeling trapped by Chase's hardening gaze.

'It will be soon,' he said smoothly, his brilliant eyes dark with determination.

Under his unblinking surveillance Alex felt her pulse begin to race with fright. Chase went absolutely still, his eyes never moving from her face. They might have been alone for all the notice he took of anyone else.

Saving the moment from getting completely out of hand, Enid said, with surprising humility, 'I wouldn't dream of organising the wedding without your advice, Miss Marshall. If it's to be in Sydney, then I suggest you follow us there in a few days' time.'

They left after lunch, Chase with them, Aunt Harriet left behind but seriously considering taking up Enid's invitation.

Mrs Young was sorry to see Alex leaving so soon after the announcement of her engagement. 'The whole of the north's on about it. Everyone's excited—the talk's never stopped.'

'Talk?' Alex queried.

'The transceiver, you know. It's a pity you're going,'

When it was time to go, Alex felt so too, but it was too late to change her mind. She hadn't thought it would be such a wrench, and she found herself wishing painfully that Chase had loved her. If he had, she could have remained here for ever, with no thought of leaving.

The journey to Sydney seemed to take twice as long as it actually did. They travelled swiftly and comfortably in Chase's executive jet from Brisbane. Alex, aware that he watched her closely for signs of nerves, made herself sit without flinching. The tenseness in her face might have betrayed her, but he said nothing. Perhaps he was as conscious as she was that her extreme pallor had little to do with her flying so soon after an accident. He had, in fact, spoken very little since breakfast, and Alex wondered if he mightn't be secretly planning to get rid of her, in spite of what he said about getting married as soon as possible.

In this muddled state of mind she arrived in Sydney. At the airport they had difficulty in avoiding a horde of photographers and, in order to escape, were forced to give in and pose for several shots. As this hadn't occurred to Alex, she felt shattered, while Chase smiled obligingly and muttered under his breath—what else had she expected? He seemed willing to tolerate such an invasion of privacy. He even nodded agreeably when one of the reporters asked if it were true that Alex was only nineteen, but immediately afterwards he whisked her from under their noses to the car which was waiting.

Enid, having monopolised what conversation there had been on the way from Brisbane, asked Chase to stay with them. The house was large—they had enough spare rooms. Alex was glad, however, when he refused. He was grateful, but he had his own flat and could work better from there.

Catching the relief in Alex's eyes, his own hardened. As she looked at him, Alex felt at an immediate disadvantage, suddenly realising she was dealing with a man who had had his own way most of his life and who certainly wouldn't change. If she proved a challenge, it wouldn't be one that amounted to much, one way or another!

Her parents faded from the hall, leaving them to say their farewells in private, Chase having also refused a drink. There was a dangerous, bitter light in his face as he stared at her. 'Any other girl but you might have been willing to spend a couple of hours at my flat. It's not that late, but I won't even ask you. I'll give you a ring in the morning.'

'If you like,' she said woodenly, keeping everything under control.

Again, as at the airport, he muttered something less than complimentary under his breath, his breathing harsh. 'I do like, and you'd better,' he snapped out tersely. 'We have to make plans, remember?'

'You mustn't let me take all your spare time,' she said jerkily, driven to provoke.

'Who else do you suggest I give it to?'

'I'm sure there are others more deserving.'

Chase's eyes glinted dangerously as he bent suddenly to find her rosy mouth. Without much pressure he rested his lips on hers, as though inviting her to take the initiative. When, with a small gasp, Alex drew back, he smiled thinly. 'I know other women with much more warmth. I might just give one of them a ring.'

'Do that!' she whispered defiantly, refusing to look at him as, with an exasperated sigh, he left her.

Anna, the old family retainer who had followed Enid from England, was waiting to welcome Alex home. 'A proper fright we had!' she shook her grey head. 'But I did say you'd be safe enough with Mr Marshall. A good man you have there, child.'

Alex kissed her, more warmly than she had done Chase, and escaped upstairs, wondering at how easily he seemed to impress people. Unhappily she wished he didn't impress people at all, as it was going to make everything very difficult indeed, once their engagement was broken. She was the one everyone would feel sorry for, for losing such a wonderful man! The thing was, now that their engagement might be ended, she didn't know how to go about it. Or was it, a small voice whispered inside her, that she no longer had any real desire to leave Chase, no matter what he did? Which was nonsense, of course, she rebuked herself firmly, and the sooner she was away from him the better!

He rang next morning, almost before she was awake. Anna called her to the telephone. 'Mr Marshall!' she mouthed at Alex's sleepy face.

'I'm sorry to be so early,' he said crisply, 'but you must have been expecting me.'

'Not quite as early as this,' she mumbled.

'I want to make arrangements for lunch. Before some of your old boy-friends discover you're back and begin ringing you up.'

'I hardly think so, under the circumstances,' she replied coolly. It wasn't something she had thought of and his tone of voice made her uneasy.

Chase named an exclusive restaurant. 'I'll meet you there at one. If you feel up to it?'

'I'm feeling fine, thank you.' Then, irrationally hurt by his continuing coldness, she said, 'Do you think we should bother?'

'One sharp,' he dismissed her suggestion out of hand, impatiently.

Because her longing to see him was greater than her pride, she agreed. 'I'll be there,' she promised, with a quivering sigh.

He must have heard, for he asked tersely, 'What are you going to do with yourself this morning, Alex?'

He sounded as if it mattered to him. Of course he wouldn't want his fiancée doing anything he didn't approve of. He had a position to keep up! Alex was thinking of planning her escape to Melbourne, but decided not to tell him. Instead she said, very casually, 'Probably nothing much. And you?'

'I'll endeavour to keep my mind off you by doing some work,' he said dryly.

The reasons why his mind should be on her could be many. Most likely she irritated him and he was happier thinking of something else. Feeling swamped by misery, she stared silently at the telephone.

'Do you still love me?' Chase asked suddenly, stunning her completely.

Swallowing convulsively, she managed to give the impression of being lightly amused. 'What a question to ask a girl over the phone!'

'I'll ask you this evening.'

'Any particular reason?' Panic-stricken, she was determined to avoid seeing him this evening.

'I've just been studying your photograph in the morning press. You looked scared to death. Nothing like a girl in love. Yet there's something in your face . . .'

Love? He had never so much as mentioned it before. Why now? 'Chase,' she protested, her heart racing with fright, 'it's eight in the morning. Can't we talk about this later?'

'We can!' he snapped, in such a way that it sounded very much like a threat, harsh enough to leave her trembling, as he hung up.

All during breakfast, which she tried to eat but couldn't, Alex remembered how he had asked if she still loved him. Surely he didn't suspect anything? It would be the final blow if he forced her to confess she did. Somehow, at any cost, she had to avoid it.

She was startled by Chase's astuteness when Don Fisher called. 'Alex,' he sounded aggrieved, 'I've just heard the news. Is it true?'

'If you mean am I engaged—yes, I suppose it is.' She coloured faintly at the way she expressed it and hoped Don didn't notice.

'But—Chase Marshall!' he breathed. 'Do you realise who he is?'

'I know he's not God,' she retorted sharply.

'Alex!' Don looked hurt. 'I don't like you when you're cynical. Maybe I shouldn't have come round but, after all, I thought you were going to marry me?'

'You thought so, perhaps,' she felt suddenly too weary to mince words, 'not me!'

'Well, I had high hopes,' he insisted. 'Your mother . . .'

'She's changed her mind, too, you'll find,' Alex said dryly.

Don missed the irony of this. With a puzzled frown he stared at her. 'I don't suppose you'd have dinner with me tonight? I'd like a chance to prove I haven't changed.'

For a moment, thinking of Chase, she was sorely tempted, but knew it wouldn't be fair. No good could come of trying to solve her problems through Don. He could never mean anything to her any more—not that he ever had. 'I'm sorry,' she whispered, sending him away.

At one she entered the high-class premises where Chase had arranged to meet her. She wore a pair of cotton jeans and a casual shirt, deliberately chosen in the hope of annoying him so much he wouldn't wish to see her again that day. She looked like a beautiful sixteen-year-old, with her hair tied carelessly at her nape and a shoulder-bag slung carelessly over her slim shoulder.

With every intention to brazen it out, she approached Chase defiantly, her eyes flickering sullenly over the tailored perfection of his suit. As usual, in the city, he looked a high-powered, ruthless business man. Even at Coolabra, dressed like his men, he had the appearance of a man born to control a mighty empire. It was an image Alex resented, for it was one which promised to defeat her.

Uncertain as to how he would regard her casual attire, she paused before him. He didn't speak, but for a moment, as she met the smouldering darkness of his eyes, she felt too frightened to move.

Then, in front of a discreetly interested audience, he kissed her briefly. 'I'd better make sure, if anyone is looking, that they understand I love you, whatever you happen to be wearing.'

Shrinking from his sarcasm like a blow, Alex went quite white. His voice was so dry that she knew he had never been further from loving her.

Regarding her shocked face, he said tersely, 'You're doing too much, too quickly. I'll get you a drink.'

He ordered her a brandy, and whisky for himself. She had noticed he had been drinking quite a lot lately.

'Isn't it a bit early in the day for this kind of thing?' Alex protested, thinking she would rather have sherry.

'Not when one has problems.' He eyed her caustically.

If she was the problem, why didn't he simply send her away? Reluctantly, because Chase told her abruptly to drink it up, she began sipping her brandy.

'What have you been doing with yourself this morning?' he asked suddenly. 'Where did you go?'

'Nowhere. Don Fisher called.'

Chase's face changed. He looked positively murderous, and his grip on her wrist reflected the fact. 'Why?' he snarled.

'To see me, I presume.' Alex winced. 'You're hurting me, Chase!'

'Really!' he snapped, flinging her wrist away. 'How did he know you were back?'

The bones of his jaw could be clearly seen under his skin. Nervously Alex licked dry lips. 'He—he reads newspapers . . .'

'Alex!' Chase thumped his fist down so hard on the table that their glasses jumped and people glanced at them again. 'I've stood about all I'm going to stand from you! I won't have you talking to Don Fisher. Understood?'

That he was violently angry under the control he was exercising was obvious, but Alex felt she was fighting for her life. If she gave in to him she could lose her independence for ever. 'I have to be polite to people!'

'People, yes,' he agreed harshly, 'but that's no excuse for encouraging other men.'

'I don't encourage other men!' she cried, her face hot at such injustice. 'But what if I did—you don't own me. Nor do you love me . . .'

'I might not exactly own you,' he replied coldly, jerking her to him so savagely she could see the glittering ice in his eyes, 'but I have a legitimate claim.'

Her blue eyes froze with resentment. 'I don't know what you intend to do . . .'

'I know what I'd like to do!' he bit back, his glance sliding over her insolently, as hard as diamonds.

'I'm—I'm hungry,' she muttered feverishly, her pulses jerking. 'Aren't we going to eat?'

'If you like,' he agreed roughly, as if he didn't care whether he did or not. His eyes were fixed on her unsteady mouth, this appearing to interest him more than anything else.

'Please!' she whispered, feeling pinpricks all over. 'You're attracting attention!'

'You're getting more than your share, dressed like that,' he said cuttingly. 'See it doesn't happen again.'

Stormily, Alex jumped up, not looking at him once as they went to the dining room. He stalked silently beside her, but the air was heavy with things left unsaid. As she sat down she stared briefly at the headwaiter's eyebrows as he escorted them to a table. Mentally, she knew, they were about an inch above their natural position, as they observed her jeans.

Oh, damn everybody! she thought, in an almost tear-

ful rage of frustration. Why was everything going so
wrong? All she'd ever done was fall in love with Chase.

She was so busy trying to control her emotions, she
failed to see Davina Wilde until she paused by Chase's
chair.

'I hope I'm not intruding?' Davina smiled sweetly at
them both. 'I just had to stop and wish you well. I read
about your engagement.'

Chase stood up, smiling as Davina kissed him
warmly. Was this all part of the congratulations? Alex
wondered bitterly. Davina kissed her next—a mere peck
by comparison to the lingering passion she had bestowed
on Chase.

'Are you with anyone?' Chase asked, as she turned to
him again.

'I was supposed to be meeting my brother,' she
laughed ruefully, 'but he's just sent word he can't make
it. Actually, I was just leaving when I saw you and of
course I couldn't go without saying hello. Now could
I?' she pouted up at him charmingly.

'Why not have lunch with us?' Chase asked, without
consulting Alex.

It seemed to Alex, in her growing despair, that
Davina spent at least five minutes allowing herself to be
persuaded, and Chase another five seeing her tenderly
seated and supplied with drinks. Davina wasn't in the
acting profession for nothing, Alex decided, unchari-
table thoughts racing through her mind. It seemed
wholly unfair that Davina was so beautiful Chase never
took his eyes off her.

Bitterly Alex regretted her cotton jeans as she saw the
elegant little dress the other girl was wearing. Davina's
make-up, too, was perfection, as were the wonderful
little curls and waves in her hair. Alex was sadly aware
that all she had gained was a sense of neglect, which
afforded her much misery and no satisfaction!

Throughout the meal, which went on until she felt

like screaming, she was ignored by the other two. They talked of people whom she had never met. Some she had heard of, but that was all. Davina sparkled and Chase responded with a charm of his own. When it was over, it seemed the final humiliation when he agreed to drop Davina at the T.V. studios where she was working.

Feeling too ill to think about it, Alex sat in the taxi Chase had called for her listening to him instructing the driver to take her home.

'I'll give you a ring this evening some time,' he told her curtly, as the taxi drove off.

Blindly she gazed out of the taxi window as they sped along. Sydney, with its ever-changing skyline, its surrounding parks, suburbs, rivers and coastline, flashed unseen before her eyes. Before she reached home she knew exactly what she was going to do. Her father was away at his conference, her mother out visiting friends. Quickly she ran upstairs and packed a case. Then, slipping off her ring, she wrapped it in a note she wrote, putting everything in a thick envelope which she addressed to Chase. This she left in a prominent place downstairs, with a note for her mother.

Old Anna was having her usual afternoon nap, making it easy for Alex to leave unobserved. Without hesitation she made her way to the airport. Managing to catch a flight almost immediately, she was letting herself into the flat in Melbourne just over two hours later. She still had her key. Because of the excitement over Ruby's wedding the lease on the flat had been overlooked. No one, so far, had done anything about cancelling it. All Alex did was tell the woman next door she was back for a day or two, then she let herself in and closed the door.

She must be the only thing that had changed, she thought unhappily, staring around, her back to the door. The flat was just as they had left it. She wouldn't be staying long—only long enough to pack the few things she still had here and decide what to do. Perhaps she would go to Darwin, in the North.

Chase wouldn't follow her. In the note she had left, she had made it very clear that everything was over between them. And from the way he had been attending to Davina, she had little doubt he would be grateful at having escaped an awkward situation with so little fuss.

Trailing into the kitchen, she made herself a cup of tea. Then impatient of her continuing lethargy, she began determinedly to sort out her belongings. No time like the present, she assured herself sternly, but by nine she was so exhausted she couldn't go on. After a hot bath she would try to eat some supper, then go to bed. A good night's sleep might help her forget Chase. Surely she would feel better in the morning?

As she got out of the bath the doorbell rang. It must be Mrs Brown from next door. She had promised to look in and see if Alex was all right. Alex hadn't thought it necessary, but couldn't bring herself to snub the woman. Sighing, she reached for her silky peignoir, pulling it on as she left the bathroom just in time to meet Chase striding over the hall.

Never could she recall seeing his face so hard and white. As she halted, gasping, he snapped harshly. 'Make yourself decent, then I'll hear your explanations. I'm sure you can think of something!'

Too stunned by his sudden appearance and biting sarcasm to feel ashamed of her near-nakedness, she grasped the sash of her peignoir tightly around her, closing the gap down the front. 'What on earth are you doing here?' she whispered, trembling.

'Just searching for my fiancée,' he enlightened her. 'And you?'

'I believe I made that quite clear,' she cried, then, to her horror, burst into tears.

'Alex!' he began, then with a helpless groan he caught

her slight body to him, gathering her so closely in his arms she could scarcely breathe. 'Oh, Alex, never run away like that again. I had no idea where you were. I could only hope you were here. I've been nearly out of my mind!'

'But why?' she sobbed, clinging to him, suddenly as reluctant to leave him as he was to let her go. 'We have to face facts, Chase. It's not as if you loved me.'

'If you only knew how much,' he said thickly, 'you might realise I can't take any more!'

His eyes were bleak as he raised a hand to touch her wet cheek, watching her grimly. Then, as though he didn't trust himself to speak rationally with her so near, he pushed her from him into an armchair. 'You don't have to pretend you're glad to see me. You're upset, I suppose, because I followed you here, but I couldn't do anything else.'

Her words almost incoherent, she stammered up at him as he leant harshly over her. 'I thought it was Davina . . .?'

'No,' he said heavily. 'She means nothing to me. I was simply trying to make you jealous.' A kind of agony darkened his eyes as they glittered down at her. 'I know you couldn't care less, but there are times, Alex, when a man feels desperate.'

Transfixed by his smouldering gaze, his barely controlled emotions, Alex was unable to speak. She had never guessed he felt this way. While she had been sitting there during lunch, feeling sorry for herself, he had been suffering too. If Chase loved her, as he said he did, he must have suffered a lot, as much as she had done. Maybe more. She could see it in the taut bones of his face.

Clouding unhappily, her blue eyes pleaded with him. 'Oh, darling, I'm sorry,' she whispered, the tearing pain in her heart refusing to allow anything but the complete truth. 'I love you so much. If I hadn't been so swamped in self-pity I might have guessed you loved me too.'

'How long have you cared?' Suddenly he was very close again, his hand shaking as it savagely curved her nape, tilting her face so he could see it clearly. 'How long?' he repeated hoarsely.

'I'm not sure . . .' She could barely think with his hands burning her like fire on her bare skin. 'Before you brought my mother to Coolabra. I think I realised how much you meant to me while you were away. I was going to tell you when you came back, but when I saw my mother I seemed to go into shock.'

'You hated me for that, didn't you?' he sighed tightly. 'I only brought her there because I was convinced, after meeting her, that your fears were exaggerated. I was trying to prove, without putting it in harmful words, that once you were married to me your fears would all disappear. I hoped you would have sufficient confidence in me to realise I could protect you from much worse than your mother. It wasn't until I saw your face that I knew my plans had been doomed from the start. You thought I'd asked her to Coolabra so she could bully you into marrying me.'

Alex nodded with sudden shame. 'But something did make me stop feeling scared of her,' she confessed humbly. 'At least I managed to grow up that much. I don't think I'll ever take her so seriously again. We'll probably get on fine from now on.'

'That's fine,' Chase said grimly. 'And where does this leave me?'

Bleakly she looked away from him. 'The—the misunderstanding between us wasn't altogether because of my mother. I still thought I bored you . . .'

'Bored me?' His brows rose in astonishment. 'However did you come to believe that?'

'I overheard you saying so to Ruby. After the first time you took me out.'

He blanched with surprise. 'Oh, God, Alex, not that!'

His hand left her nape to rub ruefully over her shoulder, easing the tension from her. He sighed, as if searching for words. 'It was far from the truth. You intrigued me from the start. I said I'd been bored, simply to stop Ruby getting at you, which she might have done if she'd thought I was interested. My sister has a very sharp tongue, as you probably discovered for yourself. I said what I did to protect you, and because I didn't want you frightened off before I had a chance to really get to know you.' Suddenly his hand stilled and he stared at her, frowning. 'You thought you bored me, yet you agreed to come out with me again. Why?'

'That was why,' she explained sombrely. 'I meant to have revenge by wasting your time. I was determined I wouldn't go to Coolabra, as you wanted me to, because of Ruby, but I decided I wouldn't tell you that straight away. I suppose my pride was hurt because of what you'd said and I decided to string you along, as they say.'

'As they say. You little devil!' he exclaimed wryly, his mouth quirking. 'You certainly did that, and I can't deny you gave me some bad moments. You refused outright to do as I asked, then just as suddenly changed your mind?'

Uncertainly, Alex flushed. 'That was because my mother threatened to come to Melbourne with Don Fisher.'

Chase nodded grimly. 'So you fled—then I confused you even further by asking you to marry me.'

'You were so high-handed about it, I couldn't believe you loved me . . .'

'I wish I'd been as convinced.' His face was suddenly haggard as his eyes went broodingly over her. 'I decided it was time I married—time to think of future heirs. Anything to avoid facing the truth—that I was falling desperately in love with you. You see,' he confessed dryly, 'I've become something of an expert at surviving devastating experiences, but I'd never had to cope with anything like that.'

'I would have told you I loved you, if I'd known you loved me,' Alex faltered accusingly, her eyes tearful again as she thought of the time they had wasted, all the terrible agony.

Chase's smile was teasing but still held a hint of grimness, as he drew her up beside him. 'I think it might be a case of the pot calling the kettle black, my darling.' He put his hands to her face, shaping it tenderly, his eyes strangely pleading. 'I have to ask your forgiveness, though. I tried to force you to do as I asked, and it didn't work. The night of the plane crash I dared not come near you. My control was nearly gone. I hadn't planned that crash, you know. I would never do anything so irresponsible, but I'd told them at Coolabra I expected to come back engaged to you, and I felt guilty. All the same,' he said, thickly, 'I couldn't leave you alone. The next morning, if Drew hadn't arrived when he did, you realise what would have happened?'

'Hush!' She laid shaking fingers over his lips, her whole body burning. 'Don't you know?' she faltered, seeking honestly to share the blame. 'I have regrets about that morning, too, but they don't seem the same as yours . . .'

'Alex!' he exclaimed hoarsely, his eyes smouldering as he stared at her. 'Oh, my little love!' he groaned, taking her mouth so passionately that the fire in his eyes seemed to swallow her up in its flames. His mouth bruised her, devoured her and she clung to him feverishly. Over and over again he kissed her, while his hands parted the thin robe she wore to find the yielding warmth of her taut breasts. She could feel him trembling, making no secret of his urgent need, as he caressed her with increasing fervour until her senses swam.

'Alex,' he groaned, his breath coming in harsh gasps,

'I told your mother if I found you we'd be married to-morrow. I told a pack of newspaper reporters at the airport the same. I don't want to leave you—but you know why I can't stay.' His eyes glittered as he strove for control. 'I won't go, though, until you promise not to run away again.'

She looked at him then, feeling for one instant the stronger, trust shining unmistakably from her lovely blue eyes. 'Darling,' she whispered, a beautiful colour creeping under her skin. 'Tomorrow, Chase, I'll be honoured to become your wife, but unless you insist I don't want you to leave me. Never again, not even tonight.'

He couldn't resist her. He might have tried, but she only heard his savage, half strangled cry as he caught her painfully closer before sweeping her up in his arms. His mouth brushed her white throat, her cheeks and closed eyelids as he murmured thickly of his enduring love for her, his mounting passion cutting off every last avenue of escape. She was his woman, and he couldn't wait now to make her so.

'I love you,' Alex whispered, finding it impossible to believe she had ever wanted to escape him. Surrendering completely, she slid passionate arms around his neck, drawing his mouth eagerly to hers, as he strode swiftly with her to the bedroom and quietly closed the door.

The Mills & Boon Rose is the Rose of Romance

Every month there are ten new titles to choose from — ten new stories about people falling in love, people you want to read about, people in exciting, far-away places. Choose Mills & Boon. It's your way of relaxing:

March's titles are:

GREGG BARRATT'S WOMAN by *Lilian Peake*
Why was that disagreeable Gregg Barratt so sure that what had happened to Cassandra was her sister Tanis's fault?

FLOODTIDE by *Kay Thorpe*
A stormy relationship rapidly grew between Dale Ryland and Jos Blakeman. What had Jos to give anyone but bitterness and distrust?

SAY HELLO TO YESTERDAY by *Sally Wentworth*
It had to be coincidence that Holly's husband Nick — whom she had not seen for seven years — was on this remote Greek island? Or was it?

BEYOND CONTROL by *Flora Kidd*
Kate was in love with her husband Sean Kierly, but what was the point of clinging to a man who so obviously didn't love her?

RETRIBUTION by *Charlotte Lamb*
Why had the sophisticated Simon Hilliard transferred his attentions from Laura's sister to Laura herself, who wasn't as capable as her sister of looking after herself?

A SECRET SORROW by *Karen van der Zee*
Could Faye Sherwood be sure that Kai Ellington's love would stand the test if and when she told him her tragic secret?

MASTER OF MAHIA by *Gloria Bevan*
Lee's problem was to get away from New Zealand and the dour Drew Hamilton. Or *was* that her real problem?

TUG OF WAR by *Sue Peters*
To Dee Lawrence's dismay and fury every time she met Nat Archer, he always got the better of her. Why didn't he just go away?

CAPTIVITY by *Margaret Pargeter*
Chase Marshall had offered marriage to Alex, simply because he thought she was suitable. Well, he could keep his offer!

TORMENTED LOVE by *Margaret Mayo*
Amie's uncle had hoped she would marry his heir Oliver Maxwell. But how could she marry a maddening man like that?

Mills & Boon
Best Seller Romances

The very best of Mills & Boon Romances
brought back for those of you who missed
them when they were first published.

In March
we bring back the following four
great romantic titles.

DANGEROUS RHAPSODY
by Anne Mather

Emma's job in the Bahamas was not as glamorous as it seemed
– for her employer, Damon Thorne, had known her before –
and as time went on she realised that he was bent on using her
to satisfy some strange and incomprehensible desire for
vengeance . . .

THE NOBLE SAVAGE
by Violet Winspear

The rich, appallingly snobbish Mrs Amy du Mont would have
given almost anything to be admitted to the society of the
imposing Conde Estuardo Santigardas de Reyes. But it was
Mrs du Mont's quiet, shy little companion who interested the
Conde . . .

TEMPORARY WIFE
by Roberta Leigh

Luke Adams was in love with his boss's wife, and it was
essential that their secret should remain a secret – so Luke
made a temporary marriage of convenience with Emily Lamb.
But Emily didn't know Luke's real reason for marrying her . . .

MASTER OF THE HOUSE
by Lilian Peake

Alaric Stoddart was an arrogant and autocratic man, who had
little time for women except as playthings. 'All women are the
same,' he told Petra. 'They're after two things and two things
only – money and marriage, in that order.' Could Petra prove
him wrong?

If you have difficulty in obtaining any of these books through
your local paperback retailer, write to:

Mills & Boon Reader Service
P.O. Box 236, Thornton Road, Croydon, Surrey, CR9 3RU.

The Mills & Boon Rose is the Rose of Romance

THE STORM EAGLE by *Lucy Gillen*
In other circumstances Chiara would have married Campbell
Roberts. But he had not consulted her. And now wild horses
wouldn't make her accept him!

SECOND-BEST BRIDE by *Margaret Rome*
Angie would never have guessed how the tragedy that had
befallen Terzan Helios would affect her own life . . .

WOLF AT THE DOOR by *Victoria Gordon*
Someone had to win the battle of wills between Kelly Barnes
and her boss Grey Scofield, in their Rocky Mountains camp . . .

THE LIGHT WITHIN by *Yvonne Whittal*
Now that Roxy might recover her sight, the misunderstanding
between her and Marcus Fleming seemed too great for anything
to bridge it . . .

SHADOW DANCE by *Margaret Way*
If only her new job assignment had helped Alix to sort out the
troubled situation between herself and her boss Carl Danning!

SO LONG A WINTER by *Jane Donnelly*
'You'll always be too young and I'll always be too old,' Matt
Hanlon had told Angela five years ago. Was the situation any
different now?

NOT ONCE BUT TWICE by *Betty Neels*
Christina had fallen in love at first sight with Professor Adam ter
Brandt. But hadn't she overestimated his interest in her?

MASTER OF SHADOWS by *Susanna Firth*
The drama critic Max Anderson had wrecked Vanessa's acting
career with one vicious notice, and then Vanessa became his
secretary . . .

THE TRAVELLING KIND by *Janet Dailey*
Charley Collins knew that she must not get emotionally involved
with Shad Russell. But that was easier said than done . . .

ZULU MOON by *Gwen Westwood*
In order to recover from a traumatic experience Julie went to
Zululand, and once again fell in love with a man who was
committed elsewhere . . .

ORDER NOW FOR DIRECT DELIVERY

Choose from this selection of

Mills & Boon 🌸 FAVOURITES
— ALL HIGHLY RECOMMENDED

☐ **C271**
NO QUARTER ASKED
Janet Dailey

☐ **C272**
THE LIBRARY TREE
Lilian Peake

☐ **C273**
MIRANDA'S MARRIAGE
Margery Hilton

☐ **C274**
PALACE OF THE
POMEGRANATE
Violet Winspear

☐ **C275**
SAVAGE LAND
Janet Dailey

☐ **C276**
DARK MOONLESS
NIGHT
Anne Mather

☐ **C277**
PARISIAN ADVENTURE
Elizabeth Ashton

☐ **C278**
THE TOWER OF THE
CAPTIVE
Violet Winspear

☐ **C279**
THE BEADS OF
NEMESIS
Elizabeth Hunter

☐ **C280**
HEART OF THE LION
Roberta Leigh

☐ **C281**
THE IRON MAN
Kay Thorpe

☐ **C282**
THE RAINBOW BIRD
Margaret Way

ONLY 65p EACH

SIMPLY TICK ✓ YOUR SELECTION(S)
ABOVE, THEN JUST COMPLETE AND
POST THE ORDER FORM OVERLEAF